MOTORCYCLEMAN

RESTLESS

Phil Englehardt

GADSDEN PUBLISHING, LLC
KINGSTON, NH
2004

Published by

DONT TREAD ON ME

Gadsden Publishing, LLC
186 Main Street
Kingston, NH 03848
603/642-3192
www.gadsdenpublishing.cm
gadsdenpublishing@hotmail.com

Produced by

PublishingWorks
4 Franklin Street
Exeter, NH 03833
800/333-9883
www.publishingworks.com
townsendpub@aol.com

**This is a work of fiction. Any resemblance to persons living or dead is
purely coincidental.**

Library of Congress Cataloging-in-Publication Data
Englehardt, Phil.
  Motorcycleman: restless / by Phil Englehardt.
  p. cm.
ISBN: 0-9744588-0-5
  1. Middle aged men--Fiction. 2. Midlife crisis--Fiction. 3. Motorcy-
clists--Fiction. 4. Motorcycling--fiction. I. Title
PS3605.N46M68 2004   2003059219

Special thanks to the believers: Kate, Caesar, Casey, Marshall, Carol, Kathy, Guy, Art and all the bees at the hive.

I appreciate the moral guidance and direction from my Dalai Lamas: O.D.B., Jerry Lee Lewis, and Snoop Dog.

To the nonbelievers I wish a life full of Izod, elevator music, Volvos, and *Survivor*.

MOTORCYCLEMAN:

RESTLESS

Chapter 1: Going Home

My name is Ian, a working-class everyman who has just reached the dark side of his forties. Today is the day to review my miserable existence. Work envelops me, relationships confuse me, and Budweiser medicates me. I have three cars, I've had three wives, and I have no answers. I feel the frustration of every middle-aged, middle-classed man. All the should-haves, would-haves, and could-haves now attack my frontal lobe. I am on the verge of crossing over to the other side. I must save myself from a life of golf dates, quiet dinners, and "Law and Order" reruns.

It is time to consult my mentor. She has never failed me. Women have failed me, children have failed me, and I have even failed myself. She has always given me the answer. I head to the broken down beach community of Salisbury, Mass. Once a thriving resort, it is now a worn-down home to whiskey bars and old bikers. The one constant of Salisbury, ever since I was a child, was that a quarter could answer all of my questions. She still sits in the corner of Joe's Playland, hunched over her tarot cards, in a plastic booth. She's been through loves, businesses, and births. She has always given me a yes or no answer and I have never doubted her sincerity. I quietly raise my quarter, closing my eyes, to ask her my question. A deep psychic state comes over me. "Gypsy Woman, is it time to change?" As many times before, she shuffles her cards and within moments the answer to my eternal question sits at the bottom of a chute. She answers "yes," and now I must figure out how to remove all of the layers of life that suffocate me.

I thank the Gypsy Woman as I have my whole life, honoring her by spending the next few hours playing skeeball and sitting in bars that have carpet for wallpaper. As the tall necks accumulate, I begin plotting my next move. I always find it hard to extract myself from my honky-tonk home, where three generations of my family have spent overnights in the local police station. Salisbury is my addiction. When I'm sitting at the Normandy Lounge, I watch my brethren strut by the door and I want to be one of them: broke, restless, and drifting.

I take my good buzz and my personal contentment and begin the process of moving ahead. The first stop is where it has always been: to look for a ride. The world has changed a lot since the last time I owned a motorcycle. There are no more grease-filled shops to fulfill your fantasies, only glossy showrooms with expensive boy-toys. Before I can realize an old dream of the perfect road bike, I have to fight my way through extended forks, fuel injection, and a variety of sleazy salesmen. As I direct them to what I need, I feel their growing disdain for my choices. Luckily, out of the corner of my eye, I see a truck dropping off a handful of police bikes. The law's choice of motorcycle is a Road King. She doesn't look like much with all the cop crap on her but I see past her blue lights and sirens. I see a beautiful, strong woman with hips that won't quit. Once you turn her on she growls at you like a Bourbon Street barmaid. She is everything I've ever wanted. I tell the unimpressed salesman my plans to dress her down, every sticker, nameplate, and other form of advertising must be removed. She was Harley black at birth and she'll stay Harley black. I will keep her saddlebags for traveling. As they begin to strip her down, you can't help but admire her simple beauty. To honor this goddess, I give her the gift of a sissy bar as well as a nice rack. She is complete, raw perfection. I would never tire of waking up to this woman and riding her to death.

I put down a deposit on my dreams. I knew it was time to call it a day. The upheaval of my life was just beginning. To change one's existence properly, it takes long-range planning but I had done enough for now. It was time to return to Main Street and slide back into my frustration and plot my rebirth.

NOW THAT the first major step has been taken, the real dilemma will be removing myself from a world that demands so much of me. My workday always starts out the same. My ten-mile drive to work prepares me for the physical and mental beating I am about to give and receive. I own a local donut shop. I give birth and death announcements. I am the giver of the endless cup. I am subjected to the same stories day after day. But I am also the King of my own domain. As I trudge through my kingdom for my first cup of morning mud, I always get the usual greeting of "Hi, how's it going?" I know they really don't care how it's going. They only care that I wake up, show up, and drive myself to the point of exhaustion so I can drive back the same ten miles and repeat the same quest the next day. Through dumb luck and perseverance my business has grown to permanent local hangout status, giving me enough cash to make me get up each morning.

My business is in Seabrook, New Hampshire, home of a nuclear power plant, a pristine beach, and a staunch Republican clientele. In the Honey Bee, people immediately gravitate toward two enormous horseshoe bays, where the stools can fit size sixes to double-wides. Cigarette smoke rises from the bays

3

like the stacks of the factories where most of the people work. I get transients, toll-takers, temptresses, and tattle-tales all surrounding me with advice on how my business should be run. Whether it's a sugar cruller or steak and eggs, I am at the whim of my business twenty-four hours a day.

As punishing as my daily routine may be, there are many blessings. I get to see the absolute best and worst in people every day. You confront all of your demons at the Honey Bee. The woman in bay one has terminal liver cancer. Years ago I would have done anything to avoid her. Now I can go out and talk to her and even joke with her without feeling lost. I never used to be any good at going to funerals but now I don't mind at all. I make up a quick, touching yarn for the mourners. "Hi, I'm Ian. I own the Honey Bee and I just want to convey everyone's sympathy. I also want you to know how many times Jack helped other people. Sometimes it was just a ride to pick up their car or a ten spot to get them through a tough spot. What I will always remember is when one of our waitresses was stricken with brain cancer, Jack went above and beyond, helping me collect money for her last Christmas with her children. I'll never forget how compassionate Jack was with Ricki and her kids when they visited the Honey Bee the last time before she passed away. Jack taught me a lot about doing the right thing, and I'll never forget him for that."

As the family starts tearing up, my mission is complete. I am now at the peak of my storytelling talent. I neglect to tell them that Ole Jack was tagging Ricki at every opportunity. While making up a story for a funeral may be reprehensible, in my world it's almost honorable. The truth doesn't matter as much as the story.

My work has also given me a cast of characters that are always entertaining. In the world of the Honey Bee there are many different types. At any given time of the day, they all may be confined in my forty- by twenty-foot hive. I will start where all intelligent life emanates, a man called Dave Harvey. No matter what the subject, no matter what the question, an answer is always followed by a complete history of the topic. He is in at 6:00 A.M. and he lifts the stools at 6:00 P.M. closing time. Dave would do anything for you except stop pontificating. He is appropriately called the Professor.

Then there's Captain Bill Shields, a sailor from the glory days of Gloucester. He mans table number four at 6:00 A.M. to give each customer a refresher course of his sea stories. Some people think that the Captain is telling tales but I grew up in the Gloucester area, and he is the real deal. The Captain has been all over the world. He has tasted their food, drunk their rum, and run off with their women. He is the last surviving member of the *Blue Nose*, the most famous schooner in the world. They say he was the best harpoon man that ever lived. He survived the worst storm in the Atlantic's history. The 1938 gale sank more men and ships than any other storm in the Northeast. His vessel was overturned by a monster wave, and they only made it through because of courageous fools like Bill. He may be a big bullshitter but to shake the hand of the ninety-year-old seaman is to touch history. Not everyone in the Honey Bee has such stories to tell.

Another patron, Ralph, always sits at the corner of the second bay, allowing him to see all of the comings and goings. His hair is dyed jet black and he believes that Elvis is in his soul. He is the Karaoke King of Seabrook, belting out song after song at any bar that will take him. There are few words to describe his vocal prowess. My description would be he sucks. For some reason, all of the clubs love his act in some sick way. In Ralph's mind, he is one step away from Nashville and stardom, and for the period of time he is in the Honey Bee, he *is* the King.

The King is not the only nicknamed patron. There is Tobacco Joe, who owns the local cigar shop. His female friend is the "Girl with the Sensible Shoes." Blackula and his wife, the Countess, are especially rude. He is some sort of Gypsy Godfather, a mulatto brown always insisting upon pure butter on his english muffins. While his wife is equally as hard to please, the Countess received her moniker from her trusty change purse— she can hold your attention down to the last penny. There is also Binky, Clown, Grumpy, Cleopatra, Queen of the Nile, Bob the Homo, and Biker Ernie.

We have no lack of Joes, Steves, Jakes, Claytons, Ronnies, and Bills. There are no Joshuas, Bretts, or Seths. Politics is spoken and screamed in between coffee and donuts. The Honey Bee cliques are well-defined. All zealots for their cause, they find lots of like-minded company. We have the ex-marines, the *semper fi* guys. The Lock and Load Club are the NRA gun nuts. The Section 8 Club is made up of uneven-tempered Vietnam Vets. The Conspiracy Club is for people who not only believe in the usual conspiracy theories, but also share some new ones that they have made up. The absolute worst club that meets is the local Klan. Their bigotry starts quietly, but if enough rednecks happen to be sitting in the same bay, the next thing you know they're ready for a good cross burning. One of the more vocal members of the ragtag group of racists is Rotha. She is loud, abusive, and her IQ is in the finger and toe range. But what she lacks in intelligence, she makes up for in looks. She has a passion for spandex. Her hair is like Velcro. She drives a Kia. And she has never held a job for more than a week. I describe her as "Rothalicious," my big all day sucker. She detests me and I detest her. These people are all part of my fourteen-hour day. I'm on my feet for every one of those hours. My only respite is at the very end with a 'Boro and a Bud, surveying the damage that has been inflicted on my dreams. As I head out the door the phone rings one last time. Cursing it with the usual "fuck you," I always pick it up like a mechanical drone. Instead of the typical donut or pastry question, I hear a familiar voice.

"Duke, what's happening?" I recognize my old hometown running mate's voice as well as the name he tagged me with.

"Rick, what's going on?"

"We're having a card game, small stakes. I was wondering if you wanted to come."

"Hell yeah!"

"It will be this Thursday night 6:00 at my house. You know there aren't that many of us left."

"I know. I'll be there, save me a seat."

"See ya then. Take care, Duke."

"Later." I put down the phone and start drifting. I realize it has been twenty-five years since I left home.

DRIVING HOME that night, the Trooper was on mental cruise control. As I light up the driveway on this cold March night, I think of all of the major decisions I've made in the last few days. I'm glued to the seat with all of the questions that I have no answers for. Am I losing my grip or is my destiny someplace else? I see the lights of other cars pull up their driveways. Could they be asking themselves that same question or am I alone in my confusion?

Walking up my steps, I've always felt that my house was too good for me. The neighbors are too nice, their kids too smart, their careers too accomplished. The only way I could match them is with my big Greek Revival. Antiques, Persian rugs, and computers were all part of my attempt to get along in their world. But at the end of the day I was still working at the Bee while they were sitting on planning boards. They had weekends by the lake. My weekends were spent slinging hash and making donuts.

I stumble into the house and receive my usual greeting from my wife, Emily.

"Hi, Hon, how was your day?"

"The usual but I did get a call from one of my old friends from Essex, Rick Means. He invited me to go play cards with some of the boys."

"Are you going to go?"

"Yeah, what the hell. It's been forever. It's this Thursday. Can you keep busy without me?"

"Actually I could probably go work on my thesis with Professor Johnson."

"That sounds okay. How is that old egghead?"

"Don't be an asshole."

"I'm sorry but he's always reminded me of Dr. Phil. I wonder if you'd ever catch Johnson kissing Oprah's fat ass. Pucker up, Buttercup."

"By the way, I got an interesting call today. It was from Seacoast Harley. They said all of the paperwork is ready for you. What the hell is that all about?"

"You know that dream bike I always talked about? I bought it."

"Great." She looked up at me from her normal perch with her faithful companion, Caesar, next to her. She named the dog after the famous Roman Emperor but all I can think of is salad dressing. Besides, he gets a lot closer to Emily than I do. He is a purebred Sheltie, like Lassie with dwarfism. He struts around like some noble beast. I put up with Caesar because he's my surrogate for most of the day. But like any territorial animal, I like him to piss off when I'm roaming my turf. Emily not only loves the dog, she is also addicted to her own personal growth. Whether it's through meditation, education, or late nights mesmerized by the glowing screen of her computer. She seeks what most females never find: contentment. Now I find myself wearing those shoes. She needs to find inner peace. I long for freedom from the shackles of my slave master, my life. This is all too much for one day. I take leave of Emily, Caesar, and all of the quiet turmoil and retire to my temple where I am the Zen Master. My barn is my sanctum, a big tree house where males still rule. Among the tools, memorabilia, and empty Bud cans, I've carved out a berth for my newest companion. She will be the final touch to my secret place. Looking back at the house, the ghostly lights of the iMac are now on. Emily's fantasy world is in full swing. That is my cue to go click myself to sleep.

FOUR-THIRTY on a March morning in New Hampshire is as depressing as it gets. No sign of life except the hum of cars going to their work of choice. Mine is the restaurant business. I was born into it. While I claim that I hate it, I love the tension and physical nature of the job. It's taken me years to figure out how to make a good living as an owner. After many failures, I have developed rules for success. Number one: Work only with people that you like. From my donut maker to my waitresses to my bread salesman, I like the people I work with. This can work against you when people have problems but in the end you enjoy your job more surrounded by people you can stomach. Number two: Restaurants are like football. Learn to win! I am the quarterback of my football team. I lead by example. Most days, I open the door and clean bathrooms before I lock that same door over half a day later. I've trained myself to never be outworked or outthought. Every movement has six reasons. The customers are my fans: if I stink they will boo me. The team around me will respond to my leadership. If they don't, I make

9

them free agents that day. Other restaurants have other quarterbacks that want your fan base. Personal preparation is the key. This is not only hard work but discipline.

As I pull out of my driveway each day, I feel like a Clydesdale. I begin with a slow trot. Steadily, as the day goes on, I pick up speed and by the end of the day I am at a full gallop. Then it's back to the barn for oats, hay, salt licks, and sleep. Like all good animals, I have a day off to refresh my legs and my spirit. My day is Thursday. Today is Wednesday so I make sure I kick out enough product to keep pastry cases full, accounts satisfied, and enough homefries, ham, and roast turkey to feed the Seacoast. Rollie, Wanda, and Cindy cover on my day off. When all is ready to go for Thursday, I get out of Dodge for a night out with Emily. We don't ever make plans on a Wednesday night but tonight is a little different. I still haven't explained my dream bike. There was no long discourse about the pros and cons, the price, or the motivation. Since the motorcycle will be arriving next week and I'm going to play cards with the boys this Thursday, I'd better placate Emily with some quality time. This would include dinner and giving her my undivided attention about what's going on in her life.

I make reservations at the Black Cow in Newburyport, a yuppie haven just over the Massachusetts line. She loves the Black Cow's view of the harbor. The crowd includes doctors and lawyers, and the women all look like Martha Stewart or Jennifer Aniston. Pretentious would be much too kind a description for the Cow, but they have a good bowl of nuts at the bar and they ice down all of their bottled beer. The reservations are for 6:30 so I can spend some quality time at the bar before they seat us. This also could present an opportunity. If enough wine is poured at dinner and I can excuse my lack of communication, I stand a good chance of getting laid. Emily is truly beautiful. She has jet-black hair, a rich face. Her frame is tall and strong. Her breasts are perfect. Since I've been with Emily, lovemaking has always saved us from our different lives.

When I get home, Emily is already in the shower, readying herself for our date. I take some time in the Temple to structure my thoughts for the evening. One thing Em is not is dumb. She must instinctively know there's a lot of distraction boiling inside me. Em will slowly grill me like Columbo when given enough time. A quick shower and shave and I painfully put on the normal clothes that I hate so much—khakis, Hushpuppies, and a collared shirt. I feel like my body is in prison. After further review in the mirror, I dump the collared shirt in favor of a black turtleneck. I add a cowboy belt and replace the Hushpuppies with shit-kickers. This is about as cleaned up I get without resorting to desperate measures. As I walk downstairs, Em is in the bathroom slapping on war paint to appease the phonies we will be seated next to for the evening. Her face has never needed the packaging. Her white teeth and her smile have always attracted people to her. As she exits to the living room, I can't help but notice how elegant she is. On nights like this, I always feel she is above me socially and emotionally. While this may be true, I control the physical and financial aspects of our union. I do notice she has a touch of lace showing, covered by a tight black blouse. This is a sign that she wants me. The only problem could be communicating during dinner and not breaking out in full fighting mode. Before we go out the door, I tell her how beautiful she looks. She returns the compliment by telling me I look handsome, excusing my combination of clothes that threatens logic. We jump in her Volvo wagon and keep things quiet on the way to dinner. About halfway there, she starts.

"Ian, how come you didn't tell me about the motorcycle?"

"You know I've wanted one for years. We looked at the same bike when we moved up here. To be honest, I just felt it was time. I'm a little bored with work, golf, yard work, pool routine. This might be a nice diversion for us. Remember we used to ride years ago? You might enjoy it."

"You say you're bored with the routine. Does that include me?"

"Of course not."

Before the conversation takes a bad turn, we both take a time out. The answer to the question we both know is yes, but we will never admit it.

WE ARRIVE at the Cow and can't help walking down to the Newburyport harbor. The icy March moon lights up the water and the shimmering lights of the houses create a Kincade-like dreamscape. As beautiful as this place is, the late winter dampness makes us both eager for the warmth and food that awaits. The hostess tells us we are about twenty minutes early. She directs us to the bar of rich oaks and brass. I've already decided on my elixir but Emily in her best uptown voice asks the waitress for a wine list. After what seems like an eternity, the waitress comes back and Em is still confused. Then comes the moment of decision. Em asks if our waitress, Suzanne, can recommend a Cabernet. The attentive Suzanne sees she is struggling with the heavy-bounded twelve page book of wines and tells Emily that she believes the house Cabernet is excellent. We finally get to order. Mine is Royal on the rocks and a Bud tall neck. Hers is an exquisite Cabernet with great bouquet probably poured out of some gallon jug with a screw-off top. The pressure of ordering our drinks is only a prelude to starting our evening conversation. I ask her about school. Em interns for Professor Richard Johnson, head of the Archeology Department at the University of New Hampshire and is in line for an assistant professor position as soon as she completes her doctorate.

"I've been busy but not as busy as you apparently. I was totally surprised by the motorcycle. I thought this was one of those things that might fall by the wayside."

"You're the one always pushing me to live a dream. This is one, and now is the time. I don't want to be some old fool with leathers and a bad prostate. Besides, with the Bee taking more of my time, this could be a good release. I can enjoy my ride any time of day or night. I've liked the golf league and my writing but I feel myself becoming a little stale."

Emily looks distressed. "I understand not being in the golf league but you're not thinking of giving up your newspaper column?" I see Emily is getting anxious. Like a lot of people, change is a scary concept to her.

I give her the answer she wants to hear. "Of course not. I love my column. It's my artistic release." Sometimes lying comes easy. I've always had a knack for it, complete with poker face and total disregard for the truth. In this case, I'm still confused about my own feelings. If I radically changed my life, Emily would no doubt be a part of that change. The fact is I still love her. She has helped form the life I now have. And it's not all that bad. Dinner arrives and saves me from anymore soul mining. Food, wine, and sex are now on the agenda. Conversation is now middle-class muted as we devour our choices for the evening. The meal is always overpriced but great. The bottle of wine is just about empty and we didn't kill each other. The chatter for the rest of the evening is about the dog, the spring flowers, and a tune-up for her Volvo. She also brings up a trip to Nova Scotia for an archaeological seminar with Professor Johnson and other department people in June. I give her the usual "how much" and "we'll see" but her reservation needs to be in next week. By this time the food and wine have done their job and there is only one more mission to complete.

As we abandon the home of the beautiful people, none of them can hold a candle to Emily. I follow that perfect round ass towards the door and as my custom, I grab it in sight of all the swells. I stop Em before the exit and notice that the coatroom door is open but not in use. I pull her towards the dark hallway with the excuse of grabbing my jacket that I already have on. The room is empty and pitch black. I close the door and explain to Emily how much I want to fuck her right here. She says, "What if somebody comes?" "That's the point. It might even be you." Emily laughs and we take a long kiss among the clatter of glass, the light roar of people out for the night. I drag the overstuffed chair in the corner and place it against the door. There is no protest left in her. She drops into the chair and stretches to help me slide off her skirt. I start at her feet but quickly work my way up to my furry dessert. For the next five minutes, I am allowed to pray at the altar of Emily's warm womanhood. I am totally oblivious to the crowded restaurant that in some strange way we were both performing to, until the noise of the door trying to be opened. Then the voice of an elderly woman saying, "She said the ladies' room was down here." There was one second of dead silence. Then in my best boss baritone, I informed her that this was the office, the ladies room was back across the other side of the lobby. She thanked me and slowly walked away blabbing about whether the waitress told her right or left. Our intruder made us even hotter. It was now my turn for the chair and Emily made me feel right at home. I was now the patient and she was the oral surgeon. There is no better delight than feeling Em's beautiful tits bouncing off my knees while she sucks me into heaven. Before I reach the holy gates, I grab her and pull her on top of me. The pace has now quick-ened and Emily is riding me like a western saddle. Like all good cowgirls she knows some riding tricks. Lifting herself up, she turns around and grabs one of the sturdy coat hangers for bal-ance before she engulfs my manhood again. In our little room we are now playing to a symphony of noise. The groans, the chair smashing against the door, the crash of the coat hangers. It was all too good to be true. She informed me the time had come and I obliged. She laid face down on the chair to give me the perfect position for deep penetration. With long, slow de-liberate strides, I waited for her sigh and the warm wetness that reveals her orgasm. My job is to wait for the timing just after she has visited her Dalai Lama. She was right on cue and it was my turn to explode. I lathered her cave with my white honey but saved just enough for the base of her spine to use as mas-sage oil for a relaxing ass rub. We now were both cooked. And after a few last licks, we knew it was time to go. The smell of lovemaking was distracting as we fumbled to put our clothes on. We both felt the buzz of contentment as we slid the chair away from the door. As we headed towards the exit we began to laugh at each other's disheveled appearances. I was particularly fashionable with my turtleneck inside out and dew drops dot-ting my trousers. As she giggled, I felt obligated to point out the pockets on her skirt were no longer functional since it was on backwards. Like two love-drunk kids we laughed our way out to the car, receiving gawks from the dimwitted yuppies since we were breaking the Newburyport "speak in hushed tones" ordinance. As we hit the road, the piercing moon was asking me why would I want to change anything. On this cold March night, for one brief moment, I remembered how I got here. I created my world of discontentment, but tonight there was none. The only quiet question I kept asking was, for how long?

WE PULLED into our driveway after a perfect evening. The doors of the car shutting alerted her faithful companion, Caesar, that his queen had arrived. Emily and I are both in contentment land. She assumes the position of God/Queen on the couch, surrounded by books, the canine, and Haagen Daas. I crawl off to bed hoping for a doubleheader but with the smell of our lovemaking still fresh, I fade off into a coma. It is rare for me to sleep past 4:00 A.M. but the cool bedroom and the night before leaves me in a cryogenic state till almost 8:00 A.M. Emily is already up in her office preparing herself for school. She has no problem fitting into the world of academia. She even morphs her looks for her other world. Her school colors are browns, greens, and blacks. Pulling back her hair gives her a more intellectual, European look. We share a Java and some small talk before she leaves for her day of buttering up her Professor. Emily reminds me to enjoy myself at the card game but be careful. She puts on her best Joe Friday about what time I might be home, excessive drinking, pot smoking, and all the possible combinations. I remind her I'm going to Essex to play cards, not running off with the Colombian Drug Cartel. Emily says she'll wait up and I promise not to be too late.

Right before she goes out the door, I say "Enjoy your other Johnson today."

Emily gives me that look and retorts, "Ian, you just don't know dick about Dick."

I've always enjoyed poking fun at the Professor's name, Richard Johnson, at times referring to him as Magic Dick, the Big Johnson, or Professor Tool. As funny as his name might be, his accomplishments in archaeology are quite famous. He is a world traveler, working on some of the world's most prestigious digs. The professor is fluent in Arabic, French, and Swahili. He lectures all over the states as well as heading the archaeology department at the University of New Hampshire. Professor Johnson recently separated from his wife of twenty-five years. The story goes he was tagging the wife of a chancellor at another small college in New Hampshire. These stories of lust are common in the ivy and brick of the Northeast college elite. Being a tenured professor is akin to winning the lottery—this leaves you plenty of downtime to pursue other interests.

As EMILY PULLS out of the driveway I start getting my shit together. With the game starting at 6:00 P.M., I thought I might go back to Essex early and check out some old stomping grounds. Needing all the quarters I can get for the game, I step into Emily's office to raid her change bucket. On top of the bucket cover is a small book with no writing on the cover. Being the curious sort I go right to the bookmark. I assumed this was one of Emily's bizarre self-help books, but what I end up finding is her personal journal. Knowing this is not my world to enter. I attempt to close the book, but the first sentence has caught my eye.

> *Richard is pressuring me for more of my time and emotion. I can't say I'm not tempted. He is so much the opposite of Ian. Life with Ian is always on the edge. Sexually we've always worked well but his edge cuts both ways emotionally. Sometimes I feel so detached. I wonder if he even knows I'm alive or what my life is like. He allows me to grow but doesn't seem to want to be an active participant in that growth. Ian is a good man, strong-willed and a good provider. I've always waited for him to give me the thing I want most: attention. Maybe I've just stopped waiting. Richard is slowly becoming more than a mentor. If I could only bottle Richard's spirituality and caring nature and slip it into Ian's evening Budweiser I would probably have the man of my dreams. Last night's date with Ian is why I love him so much but today I get my soul pampered by Richard.*

That was the end of the passage and the beginning of my anger. I wonder if finding the journal was an omen to let myself be free of Emily or was it the other way around? Years ago this news would have crushed my malehood but now all I can think about is reshuffling my deck. So fuck Emily and the Professor.

I collect my change, a fresh deck of Players, what was left of my pride and hit the road for home. The jumble of thoughts make it hard to drive but the road has a way of soothing the soul, especially an injured one. My momentary anger is soon replaced by the intense memories that I will relive by going home.

Essex is a small community of about 3,500 people on beautiful Cape Ann in Massachusetts. The town is famous for building the world's fastest and best clipper ships during the mid to late 1800s and up to the beginning of the twentieth century. As the sail gave way to the engine, the industry dried up and the town slowly began to change into what it is today. It is now a tourist haven of upscale antique shops and restaurants.

Essex is also the home of the world's best clams. Woodman's is the big restaurant of the town, employing about one fourth of Essex at one time or another during the year, between clambakes, clam diggers, and family. Not much of the town escapes their dynamic. The Essex River is more of a big creek that runs out to the backside of Crane's beach, a beautiful lagoon protected from the open ocean.

While Essex geographically and historically had a lot to offer, it also had a dark small town underbelly, something I was not aware of until my early teens. My parents owned a small restaurant and my early youth was full of freedom. While they were busy trying to make a buck in Clamtown, I was allowed to create all of the childhood fantasies that I could dream up as long as I returned by dark. The late fifties and early sixties were a time when you trusted your neighbor, and most parents felt safe letting their kids roam for an entire day without a thought. I spent my days by Chebacco Lake, which was located about a half mile from the restaurant that also served as our home, with an apartment upstairs. The ample woods, lake, and ocean provided good training ground for my adolescence. My pals and I learned early about sex and booze by watching our older peers. Most of the group that I ran with had middle-class parents who were willing participants in the Dr. Spock experiment of free-thinking and little discipline.

In the name of growth and curiosity, we became like a pack of wolves. Camping under the stars, we were always testing our limits. You either passed the test or fell out of favor with the pack and might be banished. This carried over to our education at Essex Elementary, a small but excellent primary school. It housed grades one through eight. By the time you were in the sixth grade, your education level was established. You were either in the smart class or the dumb class. You had your clique all picked out and you were getting ready to emulate the graduating class. Although they were only two years older, they were already full into puberty and trying to score with anything that moved. They knew why cold beer went with summer nights and most everyone smoked cigarettes. A pack of Marlboros was a sign of manhood. They were dreaming of their first car and how to get it. In the summer of 1966, I watched as they became adults before being shipped off to Gloucester High for their first year, knowing that in the blink of an eye, I would be there. My bicycle with the banana seat would be traded for a dirt bike. The buzz cut I sported would be replaced by shoulder-length hair. Summers of childhood fantasies would turn into adult ones.

By 1968, the changeover was in full swing. The world

around us was growing more complicated by the second. JFK was gone, Lyndon Johnson was president. The Vietnam offensive was killing thousands of American boys. Martin Luther King, Jr., was assassinated, the cities were burning with race riots. I was just in the eighth grade but I knew that these events would change my path, and very quickly they did. By the tail end of my school year, I immersed myself in politics. I quickly decided that the anti-Vietnam Weathermen protesting rebel life was where I belonged. The hair grew with my indignation for authority. I proudly wore my RFK button, bell-bottoms, and moccasins.

Some of my friends thought that I was losing my grip but I felt that they had blinders on. My mentor was a student teacher, Sandra Charles. She quietly supported me with talk of geo-politics and protests. Sandra also helped me along with puberty, giving me the perfect student-teacher dreams for masturbating. I knew she understood our talks were not only mentally but also sexually stimulating for me. I think she enjoyed the thought that she was helping a confused, future radical.

As that school year was just about to end, President Johnson announced that he was not going to run for election. This immediately propelled Robert Kennedy into front-runner status for the Democratic nomination, until the night of the California primary. I was watching it on TV, celebrating, when Sirhan Sirhan shot him. That night my life changed. I no longer had hope for a new world. A cloud of darkness and doubt was now my only friend.

The next morning, Sandra called me to her office and talked to me about the terrible night and not to fear but to look ahead. She was right. I was looking directly ahead at the firmest tits that man had put on this Earth. She said that she was leaving at the end of the year for a full-time teaching position in

New York. She came over to my chair as I stood up to leave and hugged me, telling me everything would be okay. As I tipped my head to gaze down her shirt, everything was okay, including the wood that I felt obliged to press against her thigh. She let go of me and wished me the best in high school. I left her room with a lump in my throat as well as in my pants. Everything was changing so fast and I was in free-fall.

Graduation was pure Essex. The entertainment for the night was "Manuel's Black and White Orchestra" who played for the thirty graduates as we all slipped out to enjoy a cold beer or get our last feel from our current girlfriend. That summer I began working at the restaurant at night, digging clams during the day, while baseball filled the rest of my free time. There was about a dozen of us that hung together. One hot summer day we had a pick-up game of softball. A couple of the older clammers joined in and the next thing we knew beer was flowing and Manny, a notorious figure in town, sparked up a joint. I don't think any one of us didn't join in. As we all got high, Manny gave us a primer on the world of drugs. We all knew he was addicted to heroin at one time but the story goes that he cleaned up in a special hospital in New York. He was a wealth of information. As we began our assent into drugs that summer day, little did we know that there would be few of us left thirty-plus years later to relive the stories of our youth.

The next five years of my life were a blur. I can only imagine the pain we inflicted and felt to be as drugged out as we were. We sold all sorts of drugs to support our growing habits. High school became a place to meet girls who wanted to get high so we could get laid. As high as I got, my downfall was being a little sensitive. While we shared a lot of the girls, I was always confusing love with sex. I managed to maintain one long-term relationship during my high school years with the pure but ample Judy Olfson. She was my safety net. I would talk to her for hours on end because it brought me some touch of reality in an increasingly scary life. Having sex with Judy was impossible. She would not be swayed. She was going to remain a virgin until she grew up. This made no difference to me. She gave me the anchor that I needed not to drift away. I kept Judy away from my other life. I'm sure she knew about my binges with other girls but she was my stability and I was her bad boy. I never understood why, but I fulfilled a need for her. As much as Judy meant to me, my friends came first. Our town noticed our antics enough to dub us the Dirty Dozen, although there were about twenty of us. While they noticed us, they did nothing to stop us. In Essex, the town motto was to live and let live. The adults would have their high-stakes card games, whiskey drinking, and wife swapping while we were taking every drug available and mixing them with cocktails. The boys' names were Soul, Crowley, Shep, Rick, Duke, Campbell, Ape-Man, Space Ghost, Pascucci, Spinner, Jeff, Cooper, Bista, Pooley, Jughead, Hicksy, Mike, and Magoo. Of the twenty of my comrades, seven are dead, six more are walking dead, and the remaining seven have lived with the curse of watching our fun-loving youth turn into a black plague.

I also carry the thoughts of losing two sisters to the abuse and violence associated with the late sixties and early seventies lifestyle. I always try to put them far in the back of my mind. Since they both died at the age of 48, my time could be close. Even my younger brothers have nicknamed me "Next."

AS THE TROOPER chugs over the Ipswich/Essex line, I momentarily grab back my senses enough to realize how beautiful Essex still is. The vast expanses of marshland make seventy percent of the town unbuildable, so Essex will always remain a small town. The landscape is not the only thing that is frozen in time. Most of the Townies, young and old, still live the same life that they did thirty years ago. While their bodies have aged, they still set their clocks by the clamming tides. Today the tide is early so I should be able to get a good feel for my old home before the card game.

The center of activity in Essex is the causeway. This main drag connects the two halves of the town. The causeway is home to most of the restaurants. There are also a couple of marinas, a package store, and a dozen antique shops. The centerpiece of the causeway is Woodmans. Even though it is just after high noon and a cold wind is sweeping off the marsh, there are already a few homies sitting out in front of the restaurant with red plastic cups. Nothing ever changes. These are the same faces with the same plastic cups that watched my departure from town and almost from life twenty-five years ago.

As I turn down Conomo Point Road near the Essex/West Gloucester line, memories rain down. I pass a house where a good friend lived. Gary was a clamdigger, six foot eight inches, 300 pounds. We had some good times years ago. Gary is dead, his older sister is dead, and his younger brother is dead, all before the age of forty. A little further down the road is the old baseball field where we first smoked pot. The house next to the field was a whorehouse during the days of the shipbuilders. Another half mile down the road is where I met my first wife who worked for a friend who was crippled in a car crash. John lived but my other friend in the crash didn't. I know each road in this small town would deliver the same type of memories. As I reach the end of the road, I gaze out over the beautiful view as the river turns into the Atlantic.

I pull up at Clammers Beach where pickups and boat trailers litter the small parking lot. While I wait for my old friends to come in from clamming, the March sun is warm enough to sit on the tailgate of a pickup and think about the rest of my failures. I spark up a joint for a few hits to help my dream state.

Extracting myself from Essex took a couple of attempts. Although I was only seventeen years old, I was about ready to get out of high school, fulfilling the request of my parents to just get that out of the way. Death had already claimed some of my friends and there were others who seemed on the cusp. None of us was going to college or joining the military. I can't recall one of my friends having a dream. I planned my first exit from town quietly, tuning up my 1967 Triumph motorcycle for the escape. It was late April when I received my credit card diploma from Gloucester High, making my education complete. The next day I left for California with a sleeping bag, leathers, jeans, t-shirts, and four hundred dollars. The romantic trip that I imagined was quickly changed to just trying to survive. If my Triumph wasn't breaking down then the rain was falling down. All the things I took so much for granted became a struggle, from dry clothes to a shower; I was totally unprepared. Slowly, as I began to conquer each little problem and make headway in the trip I began to feel something I hadn't felt for years: personal accomplishment. Although the ten-day trip took nearly a month and a half, I began to learn survival skills that would never leave me. I could sleep anywhere. Truck stops weren't just greasy spots with rednecks, they were oases of the road where a shower, toilet paper, gas, oil, and coffee were my mother's milk.

As I became more comfortable I rode longer each day. Being clean of drugs and booze for the first time in years, I started to feel other senses, the road buzz was my favorite. There is a high you get when you drive a motorcycle over a long distance. When you stop you feel like your body is still moving. Every smell, every element that touched you during the ride remains with you. Another feeling that came back to me was hope. On a cross-country ride, especially the first one, you are overwhelmed by the size and landscape. But what really defines your trip is the people. I never knew how naïve I was, caught in the trap of my small town. As I worked my way across country, each new person I met became part of me, from the old truck driver to the black storekeeper. Every conversation started out the same, "Where you headed?" And they all ended the same way, with each new friend giving me his life in short story form. They were all trying to help me understand that my life was just beginning. I still had plenty of time ahead of me to find happiness. Every one of these people has since been part of the postcard collection in my memory.

I finally made it to San Francisco and hooked up with Howard, a good friend from West Gloucester. He gave me a place to stay while I looked for work. I found employment at an upscale eatery called the Stinking Rose. This job was easy to come by because the owner had a tendency to yell at, fight with, and fire his help. For some reason he treated me okay, and I moved into a one-room apartment in the North side of town as soon as I got paid. It didn't take me long to feel boredom creeping back in after the joy of my long trip. The cure as always was a good buzz and a woman. The first part was the easiest, a quick trip down to Haight Ashbury, which was once the peace and love capitol of America and was now Loserville. The drug culture had taken its toll. While it was still a good place to score some dope, the peace and love days were replaced by a hippie ghetto of drug dealers and ex-cons.

Finding a woman in San Francisco was painful. It seemed that everyone that had moved there was running from something. If you could find a heterosexual woman here, complications would scare you off before you could get her near a bed.

After about a dozen fruitless attempts, I finally met June. She was California hip from the way she dressed to her lifestyle. We were easily compatible in bed and both liked to head off on the motorcycle for days at a time. The closer we became, the more we both knew that it was short-term. Someday I would go back home and she would marry the socially conscious man of her dreams. I knew it was time to move on. I scraped up all the money I had left, took my last week's pay, and hit the road with my destination unknown. The road was becoming my safe haven from all my habits, but in the back of my mind I knew the true destination was home. I went down the coast of California to the border of Mexico. I had plans of making my way down to the Panama Canal. That was before Tijuana, the small Mexican border town that services the vices of the military stationed in San Diego, which is only twenty five miles away. In one night of freakish bad behavior, I lost all my money between tequila, sex shows, acid, crystal methe, and a couple of senoritas. I woke up next to my motorcycle in another border town without a clue of how I got there. I drove to the Navy base in San Diego and sold my tired 650 Triumph to some asshole for bus fare and food money. Five days in a bus gave me plenty of time to reflect on what I had learned on my trip.

After getting home, sleeping in a bed, and eating some real food, it was time to check out my home again. It was as though I had never left. No one ever realized I was gone. We lost one more of our friends to an overdose, but besides that the time warp that was Essex was unchanged. I was quick to fall right back into my old pattern. The new watering hole was the Bunghole Lounge in the back of Woodmans Restaurant. The drinking age was eighteen. I got a job there as doorman and bartender. The year was 1972 and the choice of drugs was changing in society. While pot was still a staple, cocaine, percodans, and heroin seemed to take over for the hallucinogens that I grew up with. Mushrooms and mescaline had given way to needles and disco. With no reason to stop myself I quickly learned that heroin was the best and most addictive high in the world. The path I was on was dangerous and, if not for an infatuation, I might have been one of the casualties.

One night while I was working at the Bunghole, I met my future wife and the mother of my two children. Monique was half-Indian and half-Spanish. She emigrated from Santiago, Chile, and had only been here five years. She was brown-skinned and beautiful with jet-black hair and a compact tight body. For Essex, she was exotic. It took me some time but I slowly wore her down and we began to fall for one another.

OUR FIRST love nest was a small ranch on Chebacco Lake in Hamilton. About six other people lived with us. We were all snorting and shooting everything we could get our hands on. Both Monique and I felt that we were cats hanging onto a wall by our claws. We knew a drastic change was in order to save us. I went back to what I did best, the restaurant business, and with the first paycheck we moved to Salem, Massachusetts, to escape the demons of the beautiful town I grew up in.

Our lives slowly began to change in Salem. As my commitment to Monique became stronger so did my interest in the family business. The last piece of the long-term relationship puzzle came quickly and there was one in the oven before we knew it. We weren't twenty-one years old, we were piss-poor, she was pregnant, but as I remember it, we were in love. Monique wasn't a citizen and she was married before at the age of 14 when she first arrived in America. This didn't deter me at all, but friends and family would roll their eyes. I suppose marrying an illegal South American divorcée, with a child on the way would make anybody suspect my sanity. We rushed to finalize the divorce before the baby came, but by the time we got the final papers, Monique was ready to drop. It was a chilly March day similar to this one when we were blessed with my son, Francis. Two months later we were married by a Justice of the Peace. A month after that, Monique became a citizen. We moved to a new apartment in the Polish neighborhood of Salem and our new lives began to take shape.

A year and a half after Francis, Nicole was born. Our family seemed complete even though we always struggled to make ends meet. Our next move was to Ipswich where our love reached its high point and also died an ugly death.

The apartment on Farragut Road was tucked away just a stone's throw from the small downtown. The neighborhood was Greek and their warm Mediterranean hospitality made us feel at ease in our new home. Both children adopted a Greek grandfather. His name was Samuel but to us he was Papu, Greek for grandfather. He was a man who had been everywhere, knew everyone, and had done everything. He was in his late seventies, but his energy was endless, and so was his heart. I had never met a man like him before. He could quiet a baby just by picking it up. I always believed that a young child could feel Sam's love and immediately feel safe. I could never get enough of those cold winter days when Sam and I would drink Metaxa, smoke cigars, and eat feta cheese on hard bread as he talked about the things he had seen in his life. He was a professional wrestler in the late twenties in Chicago. Among his friends were Al Capone, Jack Dempsey, and Boston Mayor Curley. After his wrestling days were over, he promoted wrestling and boxing shows throughout the East. He was only married once and he loved his wife until the day that he died. Sam was slight in stature but a giant of a man. I wish I could have learned more from him about being strong in the face of trouble.

Monique and I kept working at the family business with perseverance. With retirement closing in on my parents, we took over the restaurant in Essex. Being young and aggressive, I wanted to make my mark quickly. We built a lounge to go along with our already busy restaurant and before you could blink we were on the fast track. Maybe we were better off struggling and poor. It seemed as soon as things started to financially get better our personal life started it's long slow walk toward disaster. At first it was small reminders that she would always be very different from me because she was from a different world. My mistake was always believing that we were making our own world that could not be penetrated by the outside. The kids were in school and we had great people to look after them so we slowly had more time for us. Her need for a connection to her culture began to take hold of Monique. I viewed this as a threat to our marriage. Our love life was getting predictable and my discontent turned into more work to avoid the brewing storm clouds. Monique's frustration turned into deep depression, therapy, and medication. The good mother, wife, and partner I loved so much was now a constant battle that turned into a war. In all wars there are casualties and we left too many. My wife's first shot in the war was an infidelity with her psychotherapist. This came to light right before she took the kids on vacation to see her homeland of Chile. As hurt as I was by her screwing her doctor, she seemed to be hurting worse than ever. Her medication made her devoid of what had made her attractive to me. As she left for three weeks in Chile, I figured we would try to work it out for the kids. I kept myself busy for the first two weeks of her trip, until one night when our live-in friend and babysitter, Nadia, had a birthday. Nadia was from Copenhagen and stayed with us while she was going to school to become a hairdresser. She was just twenty. To celebrate we went out with Mark and Laurie, long-time friends and drinking buddies. The night went on way too long and ended with some good weed and some B52s. Nadia and I went home and kept the party going as we started to get deep into my marital problems. Nadia told me Monique was going back home to see her old boyfriend that she had been in touch with as soon as she got the airplane tickets. I was so mad I put on my jacket and Nadia asked me where I thought I was going.

"I'm going to get laid. Fuck that bitch!"

Nadia reached for my arm. "You don't have to go out for that."

"Yes, I do."

Nadia stepped in front of me. "No, you don't!" I knew she was right when she gave me a long, wet kiss. I never thought of Nadia in a sexual way. She was kind of a waif and a little tomboyish, but that made no difference tonight. It just felt good to fuck away my pain. Nadia was eager and willing. There was no thought of fallout, just pure sex.

Monique came back from her trip and Nadia slipped away, moving to Boston to live with a friend from school, then moving to London to work as a hairdresser. That's the last I have heard of Nadia but that night with her kept me sane, at least for a while.

It was great to have the kids back but I despised Monique more and more as each day passed. I went to couples therapy with her for about six months. It was bullshit. The fact was that our marriage was over. We just hadn't buried it yet. She began spending some nights at her mother's so she could join a Spanish musical and dance company. One night, I called her mother's house and she wasn't there. She had been out all night. I confronted her with this when she came home. She told me she had been out with her dance partner and another man partying and didn't regret one moment. I told her if she wanted to remain a family it was time to come back. This was our last chance. She laughed at me and told me that I would never understand her. That's the day our love died.

I also found out that there was money missing. My brain was on fire; all rational thought had left me. It was the beginning of June. The summer business was just heating up and my whole world was falling apart. If mental illness or total depression were ever to conquer me, this would have been the time. Acting on those desperate feelings was very dangerous.

Once, after an especially long day at work, I dragged my sorry ass in the house only to find Monique's overnight bag on the table for another of her group fuck weekends with the Spanish Cavalcade, leaving me with business, kids, and rage. I slowly walked into the bathroom where she was in the shower. We talked for a couple of minutes without any yelling for the first time in months. I'll never forget sitting there on the hamper in that small bathroom with a pistol in my hands ready to kill her. I was slowly running the pluses and minuses through my mind. Luckily for her, I was weak. My anger, although outwardly directed at her, was inwardly directed at myself for allowing all this to happen. She left for the weekend. I went to work but my head was on fire with hatred. That Sunday was Father's Day. She called and said she was coming home to cook a nice dinner.

When I got home that evening it looked like a scene out of Ozzie and Harriet. The table was set, and even the kids weren't beating up on one another. I received a chorus of "Happy Father's Day" as I walked in. For one moment, I felt like everything was normal. That mood changed quickly when Monique informed the children that they were going on a grand adventure to learn of their heritage. They would be moving in with Monique's sister and mother. They would go to school in Cambridge. "We're going to give Daddy a nice vacation but don't worry, everything will be all right."

I couldn't believe what I was hearing. This was the first I'd heard of the move. All I could think was that I should have shot that bitch when I had the chance. But it was too late. The fact was I just didn't have the balls.

We finished dinner. I put the kids to bed. I told them not to worry, that this was probably just a temporary situation. After I was done lying to them I took my wife outside for a good screaming match. After fifteen minutes of banging my head against the brick wall that I once knew as my wife, I walked down to the local Knights of Columbus and looked for someone to jabber with. But the people sitting in the stools were just as pathetic looking as me, so I quietly drank my Buds in between shots of Royal and planned my departure from the hell I had created. My ride at the time was as pathetic as my marriage. It was a big Yamaha fresh off the showroom floor. It was when they first started making Jap bikes that said "See, it looks just like a Harley, except you won't have to fix it every ten minutes." This motorcycle was another reason why the mid-eighties sucked but it was the only thing I had the keys to.

The next morning I was hung over and pissed but I knew this part of my life was over. For my own salvation, I once again packed up my sleeping bag, leathers, jeans, t-shirts, cash and my gun in case my wife tried to track me down. At that moment in time, I didn't think of all the people that my choice would affect. I could only think of my own failure. I still regret my decision to this day.

I took a long deep breath as I left. I exhaled about fifty miles out of Baltimore as the road finally started to take affect. I pulled into a neon oasis to gas up, clean up, and throw up. I sat outside that gas station all night, wondering how the fuck I got there and which way I was going to go next. It was dawn before I came to an answer. I had never been south before so that was the obvious choice. I packed up what was left of my pride and headed toward Virginia Beach, four fun-filled nights of acting like a pathetic drunk.

Virginia Beach was home to the PTL "Praise the Lord!" Empire. After four days of getting stiff, I figured it was time for a little salvation. I always had great admiration for Tammy Faye and her makeup, but her husband was a loser. Could this be my chance to lay down with those big eyelashes? As I drove by the entrance to the phony holy city, I knew the road was the only false God that I would be praying to for the next couple of months.

I SLOWLY started my march to the deep south at Kitty Hawk, down the coast to Ocracoke Island and a ferry to Beauport, South Carolina. While gassing up, I saw a hand-written poster on the building. It read, "Shrimp Boat Laborer Wanted. Call Willie at 478-3122." Something about the sign brought me to call. I talked with Willie's wife and she said he was already down at the boat. She said he was leaving tomorrow morning and that I should head down to state pier at slip 17 if I wanted to work.

The boat was named the *Miss Bea*. It was about forty-feet long and resembled the other ten boats that were lined up next to it. There was a light on in the cabin but it was tough going on this moonless night. As I approached the door I was greeted by Willie: six foot, three inches, 280 pounds, black as night, with a flashlight in one hand and a shotgun in the other. Before I could open my mouth, Willie said, "Why you here, Cracker? This is my boat."

"I talked with your wife and she sent me over about the

job." Willie slowly set his gun down to his side and with a loud laugh said, "What's a white boy like you looking to be shrimping for?"

"I need some quick money and besides, when I read your flyer, it didn't say whites need not apply."

Willie gave a big, missing-tooth smile, laughed and invited me into his cabin. "What's your name, white boy."

"Ian Payne."

"Mine's Wilson Jones, they call me Willie 'cept when we're out at sea, then it's Captain. Shrimpin' season lasts about three weeks, and we work every one of those days. The pay is $200 a week plus bonus depending on the catch. My break-even point is four ton, the bonus will kick in after that."

"Sounds good to me, Captain."

"How do I know a northern white boy like you knows a shrimp from a sea turtle?"

"I grew up around Gloucester, and crewed on swordfish boats."

Willie looked skeptical. "If you was fishin', how come you got all your fingers?"

"Look Captain, I can do the job if you need the help."

"Well, seeing no one else has applied, you got the job. We leave at five in the morning. You got any place to stay?"

"No."

"You can bunk on board then. You got any gear, Ian?"

"Only two saddle bags and a bedroll, but I could use a place to put my motorcycle till I get back."

"You can leave the bike in the storage shed near the front of the dock. Come on, I'll show ya." I parked the bike and grabbed my belongings. As we were walking back towards the boat, Willie said, "You're traveling light. What you running from, the law or a woman?"

34

"Neither," I said. "The sad truth is I'm running from myself." It looked like I struck a chord with Willie. He rolled his eyes and said, "Ain't we all."

I was beat that night and I slept like a rock. At 5:00 A.M. sharp the engines of the *Miss Bea* began their slow roar. As I crawled out of the bunk, Willie was already on deck untying us. For the next three weeks, we worked our asses off. The fishing was just okay and I knew enough so that Willie didn't throw me overboard. As the first week went by, I learned a lot about shrimp. By the end of the three weeks, I knew a lot about Captain Wilson Jones. He had spent time in prison, had been married three times, had six children, and was now one with Jesus. He didn't trust Whitey. He loved to gamble and screw on Saturdays so that he could give his life to the Lord on Sunday. Willie didn't try to counsel me. He did let me know that Jesus would always forgive me but that the hard part was forgiving yourself. I wasn't ready for the Captain's advice and as the end of our trip was near, I was feeling angry and dark. As the days were becoming hotter and unbearably humid, the boat was stinking and my soul was slowly rotting. When we finally docked, it took us a day to unload and get the *Miss Bea* cleaned up.

That night, Willie took me to his house for a great meal of soul food that his wife served up. He offered to let me sleep on the boat for a few days but my mood and mind was already on the road. I left that night headed for the deep south.

EACH DAY the weather was hotter than the day before. The whole south was drenched in humidity. It was almost unbearable riding during the day. At night, like clockwork, thunderstorms would roll in and provide a torrential downpour for half an hour. This only made things worse. There seemed to be no relief in sight from the heat.

Every chore that is difficult on the road started to become agonizing. I'd clean up at a truck stop, dry all my clothes and sleeping bag in a local laundromat, and then have to repeat that exercise the next day.

The towns and the miles began to add up: Savannah, Atlanta, and Tallahassee. Panama City was the next stop on this ride through hell. I crossed over the long bridge to the gulf resort town just as the sun was setting. The backdrop against the hazy sky and the full moon rising was surreal. I knew it was time for a couple days off of the bike and a bed. Jack's Shacks was the perfect spot, about two dozen little open door huts on the beach. After two days of jumping in the water, cold beer, and sleeping in the hammock, I started to feel human again. As the third day dawned so did a chubby. Since I began my trip there wasn't even a thought of a woman but today was different. The sun was barely up but I was already on the prowl. Three huts down there was a woman that I had bumped into a couple of times. She was the librarian type, hair pulled back, lots of books, glasses, a little light up top but the rest of the package looked pleasurable enough. I've always found this type of woman fun. The repressed uptight type usually is a wildcat if you can get them in the sack. I slowly walked by her shack that morning a couple of times, waiting for her to stir. She finally got up and started her morning routine of setting up her books by the beach chair in front of her hut. I made my way close enough to give her a 'good morning' and a smile. She smiled back and the door was open.

"Hi neighbor, my name's Ian. I'm going down to the store to get a cup of coffee, can I get you anything?"

In a nice southern drawl, she said, "No thanks, I think I have everything I need right now."

"Well, if you change your mind I'm a couple doors down

at number ten." I went down to the store and bought my usual coffee, beer, and ice and went back to my hideout to start thinking of other alternatives to the librarian. It was about noon and I was just done with my second dip and second beer when a familiar voice came up behind me. "Does that offer still stand?"

I turned to see my neighbor, her hair was now down and the glasses were gone. I forgot what offer I had made her but my answer was easy. "Absolutely."

Her name was Darlene and she was a computer geek over in Pensacola, Florida, at the air base. The next few hours we just talked in between cold beers and dips in the Gulf. She regaled me with stories of her home in Biloxi, Mississippi, and the two times she thought she had found Mr. Right. Both times she fell short of the altar. I was more than happy to listen to her go on forever about herself. However, she kept probing me about how I ended up in Panama City. I tried to explain my condition to her but I kept it short and sweet—I didn't want to scare her off.

"Darlene, you should be thankful for not reaching the altar. In my case, I married young, had two kids, and built up a nice business and life. In a matter of two years it all came crashing down—my wife's depression, infidelities, and just too much hatred for a relationship to survive. She cast me aside and I was too worn down and weak to fight. Right now I'm looking for rock bottom so I can begin to pick myself back up and go on with life again."

There was a lot of truth in short, and sweet Darlene started to tear up. I figured she would run back to her books and put her glasses back on but she stayed, only saying how sad my story was and trying not to probe any deeper. I suppose she thought, Hey, I just wanted to get laid, not involved.

We took a few more dips and a couple of more beers and

decided to go out for some dinner. We took the motorcycle. She had never been on one before because her papa wouldn't allow it. Like most things Papa wouldn't allow, once you try them you don't want to stop. That evening we traveled up and down the coastline. She grabbed a little tighter with each place we stopped for a drink. By the time we were heading back towards our huts, she was telling me that the vibration of the bike made her all wet. We fucked on the beach that night, all the hurt and frustration I had inside made it's way to the surface during our lovemaking.

The sky was beginning to lighten by the time we woke up the next morning on the beach. Darlene told me she had to leave to go back to Pensacola that day. She left me her number in case I drove through. I slept most of the next day away, between brooding about what might be next. As the noontime sun started to wane, I just sat on the beach chair looking out at the water, thinking of all the pain that I had caused my family. The rage at myself was too much so I devised a plan to let fate decide if my life would continue. Darkness had crept in over the gulf. I had a smoke and sip of beer, then went into my saddlebag and took out my pistol. I put one bullet in the chamber and spun the wheel. Two seconds later the barrel was in my mouth and I pulled the trigger, only to fail. That click that allowed me to live will never leave me.

I knew that only luck let me drive away the next morning. My trip would continue but the truth was I had to go back and pick up what pieces I could and start over. The words spoken just two days ago to Darlene kept coming back to me. I told her I was looking for rock bottom. The night before, I had found it. I rode over the bridge, heading back towards the Panhandle. About halfway across, I pulled the gun out of the saddlebag and threw it into the Gulf. I slowly made my way through Biloxi and headed towards New Orleans. Summer was in full throttle and the Delta was steaming. While the heat was unbearable, the setting was perfect for some good debauchery before I headed back north.

I pulled into a campground in Black Bay, just south of New Orleans. The snakes were docile this time of year so sleeping under the stars was no problem. The food was great at the campground diner, strictly shrimp, red beans and rice, and the music was Zydeco. Bourbon Street was in its off-season and it only deserved one night. The jazz and the hurricanes were for the tourists. The strippers were accommodating but they even blurred after a while. The real action was in the little parishes outside of the city. It was like driving back twenty-five years to a simpler time. Men still wore hats, living was so slow you thought it stopped sometimes. Blacks had a different attitude from the rest of the South. They had their own separate, more mysterious culture that seemed to mesh perfectly with the eerie, natural surroundings of the swamps. You could feel the voodoo. The revival tents were always full on Friday nights and so were the juke joints. As beautiful as this part of the country was, I knew time was running short. If I didn't return soon there would be no pieces left to pick up. So after a short week of Louisiana living, I started my long trek north. I decided to go through the heartland on the way back, taking route 55 North through Mississippi. Two days of hard riding landed me in Memphis, where I took a night to pay homage to the King.

But there was no more time for sightseeing. In four days of hard riding, I went through Tennessee, Kentucky, West Virginia, Pennsylvania, and into upstate New York. I landed twenty miles outside of Buffalo, worn and weathered. I camped out alongside the highway that night, next to Lake Erie. I had every intention of heading home the next morning.

I woke up cold and cranky. I figured I'd take in Niagara Falls before heading to route 90 East. As I overlooked the falls, for some reason I realized that I wasn't ready to look in that big mirror. I jumped on the bridge and headed towards Toronto.

It's hard to believe that Toronto is the entryway to the wild north. It reminded me of a typical American city. The only difference was the maple leaf displayed on every flagpole. I left as quickly as I could and headed northeast. I skirted the border by Lake Champlain and rode toward my final stop, Montreal.

The road to Montreal was monotonous. Of all the miles I had driven motorcycles, I never thought it was possible to fall asleep on one. About 75 miles outside of Montreal, I started counting sheep at 65 m.p.h. I woke up on a soft shoulder just in time to say "fuck!" Your first reaction is total panic. That's when you make the situation worse by hitting the front and rear brakes full force. Then comes that slow, sliding feeling as the rear end of the bike starts to kick out from under you. There is no time to think. You just lay down and wait to hear noises. I didn't hear any crunches. That was a good thing. After a minute, I shook the cobwebs out of my head and began to check my body parts. Once I realized everything was intact, I looked over at my motorcycle. Beyond dents and scrapes everything was in full working order. It really didn't make much difference. As functional as this bike was, as many miles as it had taken me, it had no spirit. It was a lot like me at the time. But it was still the only bike I had. So I picked it up, dusted it off, and continued on with the final leg of my trip.

I got to Montreal at about nine at night. I wasn't sure how many days it had been since I last cleaned myself up. I got as close to St. Catherine's Street as I could and I found the cheapest dive with a bed and a shower. The road finally caught up with me and I slept for twenty hours.

It was then time to visit my friends on St. Catherine's Street. Montreal was home of beautiful churches and wonderful French cuisine but that pales in comparison to the strippers on St. Catherine's Street. What makes these dancers so special is that they actually smile while they are relieving themselves of their clothes. This is opposed to the American variety who give you that look of disdain if you try to put anything less than a fiver in their g-string.

I tried to get my thoughts focused on the most beautiful tits and ass in North America but my mind was about seventy miles back where I came so close to having fate take my life, just when I was getting ready to go back and face my failures. Maybe someday I'd go back to St. Catherine's Street with a better outlook. I said good-bye to each and every club on the strip with a cold Labatt's Blue and a good tip for the freakiest looking girl with the best smile. I headed back to my room to pack up for the last leg of my trip.

After getting everything in order, it was 11:00 at night and I wasn't in the mood for sleep. I made my way across the street for a couple more coldies before closing time. The bar was strictly local, French-speaking. I could feel the patrons roll their eyes as the word Budweiser left my lips. You could see the bartender thinking, *With all our wonderful Canadian lagers, why does this asshole need a Bud?* The answer I kept to myself. After a while, Molsons and Labatts just suck.

My choice of brew didn't go unnoticed. A woman two stools down said, "What's a Bud-drinking Yankee doing here? Shouldn't you be down with the rest of your tourists on St. Catherine's?" Touché.

I sent her over a bottle of Canadian Ale and slid over a stool. "You sound just as white as me. Tell me what a good American girl is doing here drinking lousy Canadian beer?"

She stared at me with a sort of sad, faraway look and wondered out loud, "I don't know."

Her name was Kendra, she was from Maine, and she was taking a break from a husband who made her feel small. Kendra could take a lot, raising two kids, being the caretaker, etc. What she couldn't take was her husband, Ron, screwing the hell out of their next-door neighbor. She was asking all of the self-analysis questions. What does he see in her? Was he really that unhappy? What does she do that I didn't? The questions quickly turn to self-blame. Could I have been a better wife? What's wrong with me? Kendra was asking all the questions to which she would never find any answers. But she was just hiding from all the things she would have to answer. Would she take him back? Could they ever be a couple again? Dear Abby would recommend marital counseling. The minister says to work it out for the kids. Kendra's mom says to divorce the bastard and to come live with her.

Listening to Kendra, I realize that she is just at the beginning of her self-imposed trial, whereas, I've gotten to the point of the verdict. She is just beginning her trip and mine is all but over. After listening to Kendra nonstop for about an hour and slowly plying her with Canadian beers and whiskies, I start to tell her my tale of sorrow. I use the short version with enough self-deprecating humor and sensitivity to have a chance of getting fucked by a pissed-off woman looking for revenge. I'm well on my way when she starts to tackle shots of Tequila and begins to rant about Ron and payback. Before she falls off of her stool, I tell her I'm going outside for some air and she stumbles along with me. We sit on the wall by my motorcycle and I ask her if she wants to smoke some hash. She giggles and says she hasn't done that since high school. We take a few hits and then just sit there looking at the glow of summer on the Montreal skyline.

Maybe it was the dope, or God forbid, a conscience but I took Kendra back to my room and put her to bed. I slept on the floor. Before nodding off, I questioned my good behavior, promising myself it would never happen again. The baby Jesus must have heard my prayer. When Kendra woke up the next morning, she taught Ron the lesson he so richly deserved by screwing me. She thanked me for not taking advantage of her when she was so loaded. I lied and told her that I could never do such a thing. For the next two days, we rode around Montreal seeing the sights, each reflecting on our own mess. It was a damp early September morning when I wished Kendra good luck and made the five-hour drive to try and have a better ride with the second half of my life.

THE NOISE of the skiffs buzzing across the river brought me back to my senses. It had been so long since I'd been home. As the boats pulled up to the dock, I drove away for a little more time with my memories before the card game.

I drove back to the other side of town to check out the restaurant that I used to own. Since I left, there had been three owners. When I owned it, it was called Misty Acres. The first time I sold it, the name changed to Lee's Misty Acres. He owned it for four years before it went under. Since we carried the note on the property, I had to go back and resell it. In both cases, I had to go back with a new owner to help them revive business. It seemed like the place had a hold on me for years after I left. Every time I felt like I was forging ahead, somebody would go bankrupt and I'd have to go back and relive the nightmare. The last time we sold it, it was for cash, so that part of my life was finally over. You'd hardly recognize the place now. It's called Jan's Encore. I hear it's high-end dining, but I'll never know.

The card game is right around the corner and it's almost six o'clock. The entrance to Rick's house is like driving into the Ewing Ranch. A big stone pillar is engraved with the words "Turf Meadow." Rick's stepfather owned the big house, lots of acreage where buffalo used to roam. The children had houses on the same property, but tucked away in their own little nirvana. Even though they grew up well heeled, that didn't stop them from having the same problems as the rest of our crew when they were younger.

Rick was the most successful of the bunch. He married some Manchester money named Jules and operated a successful fence company. It's a far cry from where we started. In our teens, we started our own business called Rinky-Dink Enterprises. We cleaned garages and mowed lawns, but our claim to fame was our Sunday Beer Blasts. We would take my Harvester International pickup, drive to New Hampshire and load the whole thing up with beer. On the way back, in Salisbury, we'd stop at the Ice Company. A chute would ice down the whole back of the truck and we'd drive off to a secret location with our frosty cargo. By the time we landed, thirsty teenagers were already gathering. We also sold joints to accompany a chilled brew. Our only expense, beside the pot and the beer, was hiring Big Ern to make sure nobody clipped any of our product. He'd sit on the hood of the truck, all 300 pounds of him, with a baseball bat. I forget how much we made on those Sunday bashes, but the fringe benefits were excellent.

As I drive up Rick's driveway, I see that his house is upper-middle class big, complete with boat and truck. It's just how I imagined it. I get out of the Trooper and see Rick, his older brother Shep, and Bista standing in the kitchen. Years ago if I had walked in, we would have been sparking up a dube and sucking down a few cold ones just to get ready to deal the first hand. Now all of them are either on a diet, strictly sober, or thinking about Jesus. We no longer feel or look like we are going to live forever.

We sit down at Rick's fancy eating table. The fifth in the game is Jake, a long time clammer that I don't know as well as the rest. The conversation is adult-male superficial. In with my bag of quarters, I have snapshots of what my life had become, a picture of my granddaughter, my house, my wife, and my new motorcycle. Being a columnist for the local newspaper, I also had thrown in a couple of my pieces.

I lose the first five hands. I am more interested in starting conversations about what had happened during all these years, rather than how the steak tips were at Periwinkles. The group I had known as a wild bunch was now a mild bunch. There is some excitement when I ask Rick where his wife is. Everybody rolls their eyes as Rick goes into a quiet but constant tirade on the wife that has apparently left him. Obviously, I had touched a nerve. I guess Ricky isn't dating yet.

As the night wears on, I decide to quickly lose my money. When you live in a town your whole life, there's an undertow that tries to drag you back to the same spot forever. Some people find that comforting, but what I always thought is that it would drown me.

I know it's time to go so I give my standard baker's excuse. "Gotta get up early to run the Honey Bee." I grab my empty moneybag, the only thing left inside is the pieces of my life that I wanted to share, but nobody had asked. I say my quick goodbyes and we all lie about doing it again real soon.

As I drive away, I feel disappointed. I had hoped for a connection to my old friends but it just wasn't happening. I pull into the Falls packey for a couple of tall boys for the ride home. As I head towards the door, I hear somebody say, "Hey Duke, is that you?" I walk over to a black van and see my old buddy, Mark, sitting in the passenger seat. We were good friends way back when, until I made the mistake of getting mixed up with his girlfriend for a day. He wasn't supposed to find out about that and when he did he smacked me right in the face. I deserved it so I didn't fight him back.

Now Mark suffers from Multiple Sclerosis and he needs a wheelchair to get around. Being the tactful person that I am I said, "How's it going?"

"It's going fucking great. I'm stuck in a wheelchair and you still deserve a good beating."

"Having a tough time letting it go, Mark?"

"You haven't changed much. You're still a dink!"

Even I have rules about pissing off guys in wheelchairs. I figure it's time to cut our conversation short, besides I'm thirsty. I go into the Packey and stand there thinking to myself, what was that all about? And then I remember how much fun I had with his girlfriend, Lisa, that day. It was time to do some drinking. I reach for the blue box. If you relive your past all in one day, only Crown Royal will do. I bring it up to the register and add a couple tall boys and a pack of 'Boros. Then I'm on my way to relive one last moment before I leave town for good.

Driving about one mile, I stop at Sagamore Hill, little more than a bump on the map between Essex and Hamilton. It is home to an air force observatory. It's also where the great Indian Chief Masconomet was buried. His headstone stands as a monument to a different time. He died in 1659 on the land that was left for him by the puritans after they stole his tribal homeland for twenty dollars and a box of rocks back in the early seventeenth century. The names Whipple, Wise, and Smith are more important to this area in the historical sense. These men are the reason my mentor Masconomet, Chief of the Agawams, the Pentuckets, and the Chebacco tribes, is now just an after-thought, buried on an eight-acre parcel that the white devils allowed him to keep.

Sagamore Hill is also home to the best memories of my youth. The house I grew up in overlooks the hill. It was littered with arrowheads, old wagon wheels, and enough imagination for two childhoods. At eight years old I stumbled across the headstone of Masconomet. This hidden treasure has always been a secret memorial adorned with dreamcatchers, beads, feathers, and other offerings given to the spirit of the Chief. I delighted in bringing friends up to the top of the hill to meet the Indian ghost. I got into the habit of leaving an offering and taking a good luck charm when I visited.

The last time I was there was in the summer of 1970. I was walking down the street thumbing a ride when I bumped into Lisa, my friend Mark's girlfriend. She was also tight with my girlfriend, Judy. Lisa asked me if I was busy and if I had time to talk. I said yes and we walked up on some rocks at the base of Sagamore Hill and sat down. I asked her if she wanted to smoke one up, so we did. I just lay there with a good summer buzz while Lisa began to talk about her father. He was in the air force and worked at the observatory at Sagamore Hill. They were being transferred. She told me not to tell anyone, especially Mark. This was the longest Lisa had ever lived in one area in her life and she was devastated at the thought of moving. As she started crying, I rubbed the back of her neck to try to relax her. That's when she told me that there were things that she wanted to do before leaving. As we sparked up another joint I asked her what she wanted to do before she left. Lisa smiled and asked if I could take the day off with her. We finished the joint and I told her I didn't have anything planned. I wondered out loud what she was thinking. Lisa made me promise that whatever she told me and whatever we did would be our secret. I agreed and she said, "I really like Mark, he's real kind to me but he's not real romantic. Judy keeps telling me about the things you guys do and I'm jealous."

I am now in full prayer to the pussy god hoping that Lisa is coming on to me. "What has Judy told you?"

"She said that you scare her. She says that you want to have sex in public, lots of oral, enjoy being nude and she is always waiting for the next weird thing you'll want to do."

I turned a little red-faced. "I don't consider myself weird at all. Judes just a little uptight."

Lisa and I lay on the rocks and kissed without saying another word. A long breath later, Lisa whispered, "I'm going to miss this place, there are so many things I haven't done. Take the day with me. I want to experience some of those things before I leave."

"I'll never tell anyone." At this point, I didn't care who she told. This was a sixteen year old's dream come true.

Lisa dressed like the perfect little hippie girl. She had long brown hair, pulled back, with a light brown Indian shirt with little mirrors on it. Her bellbottom jeans were tight enough to expose a small but round ass. Sandals completed the package.

We kissed for another long spell and I asked, "What's your pleasure?" There was some pressure to live up to my billing, so rather than take the lead, I sat back and let the young exotic, erotic creature take me into her dream world. Her first request was to just be naked and talk. I had never attempted this before. The only time I was naked was skinny-dipping while camping with Judy. I always had the urge to be without clothes although I could never get her to join in. The only other time I was naked in front of someone was trying to get laid. It must be an old Puritan law about intercourse only in the dark.

We sat directly in front of each other in a lotus position, leaving nothing to the imagination. I tried to transfix my eyes with hers but being rock hard and trying my best to actually carry on a coherent conversation, I started to get male confused. After about fifteen minutes of yakking about all our insecurities with our bodies, it became more comfortable. We kept talking for the next hour. Lisa asked me about masturbation, how often, what thoughts go through my mind, when I'm ready to come. As I'm talking, I say "what the hell" and show her hands on. My *Naughty Neighbors* magazine was not necessary for this moment. With her sitting across from me I finished almost as fast as I started. Still in the lotus position, it was now my time to watch. She didn't disappoint. Her play by play was delightful and I learned about that little nub of heaven for a woman called the clitoris. You could see her melt into her personal orgasm when she concentrated on her little love button. To my surprise, she was done almost as quickly as I was. I learned more that one day about women, sex, and fun than I would the rest of my life. We continued the day until dusk in total nakedness and enjoyment. We saved the best for last, we made our way to the headstone of Masconomet. This provided the perfect spot for Lisa to stand, allowing me to enter her for the first time all day. It was like we were both making an offering to the Chief.

As I APPROACH the rock to pay homage to my old friend, I can still smell the sweet innocence of Lisa and that perfect day. I drink to Lisa, I drink to my chief, and most of all I drink to wash away those memories of my trip back home. The March air is cold but I don't feel it. Now all I think of is plotting my next trip that will be the last.

I stare at the headstone, hoping for answers about how to

untangle all the parts of my life that grip me. Emily is the only one in my life that I am true to and now she is feeling the pull of another man. My business, that I curse daily, is still something that I love, but there will be no time left if I wait.

My trance, my Royal, and my memories have now carried my soul into the early hours of the morning. I leave a small blood offering to my chief, as is my custom. I take a small string of beads for the new motorcycle for protection. I then limp back to my Main Street home and an angry Emily. I just put on the blank stare, explain nothing, and catch a few hours sleep before I start the long painful process of resurrecting my life.

Armageddon Days

THE NEXT MORNING my hangover was brutal. It had been a long time since I had a good drunk. Emily read me the riot act before leaving for work. There was no explanation for my bad behavior but it felt great. I was clamming up on Emily on purpose, to piss her off. I was dying to whack her around about Mr. Fucking Sensitive but I just took my scolding and headed off to work.

Pulling out of the driveway, I notice the clock. I was real late. In the nine years that I've owned the Honey Bee, I've always been on time. I totally forgot that this was my day to open. I am now two hours late and running on fumes. As late as I am, I take a long, slow cruise to work to get my bearings. The ride is much too short. I should've kept on going. Like the drone that I am, the car drives into the parking lot and stops in the all too familiar spot. I crawl out of my seat like a ninety-year-old and stumble in the back door. I am immediately greeted by three employees looking for an explanation, two sales weasels looking for green and a two-page to-do list. Before I got there I think they were all huddled around picking straws to see who was going to be the asshole to state the obvious.

"Hey boss-man, you're running a little late, aren't you?" That's all it took for me to go off like a Roman candle.

"Well, thank you Mr. Fucking Timex." I could see everyone ducking in anticipation of my next volley. The sad fact was that I just couldn't muster the energy to start ripping into all of my inquisitors. I told the two salesmen to screw and come back when my eyes would allow me to write a check. I slipped into my apron and propped myself up behind the grill. It used to be so easy when I was younger. I'd pull an all-nighter and work the whole next day, no sweat. Now I look like some guy who stepped out of the homeless shelter.

As pathetic as I look and feel, my coworkers know all the moves to get me in gear. Regina quietly brings me the coffee I so desperately need. She wears a little grin, enjoying the condition I'm in. She has been at the Bee longer than I have. I don't know anyone that could outwork her, although I try. Her warm nature and German upbringing is the perfect combination to work a tough crowd.

Out of the corner of my eye I catch my night baker, Guy, doing his quiet tiptoeing. This routine is exclusively reserved for when the boss-man is tired or pissed. It's like he wants to give me a hand, but he wants to stay far enough away in case my head explodes. While I was in dreamland this morning, Guy stayed and filled my shoes. As time goes on, he does a lot more of this. Guy grew up hard in the streets of Lawrence, Massachusetts, an old mill town on the Merrimack River. Lawrence is home to a variety of non-working immigrants, white trash, and boarded-up buildings. You would think Guy would have a hard edge to him but instead it's the exact opposite. He is thirty-one, hard-working, middle-class smart, and a little too nice. He's six feet one inch and he looks like an Iowa farm boy. Guy's family and friends always seem to take advantage of his generosity. Guy's always busy doing something for someone, even his ex-wife, Janet. I never say more than two words to either of my ex's, while Guy still gives a helping hand whenever she comes crying.

Today was my day to take advantage of his good nature. "Hey, Guy-man, grab me a couple racks of eggs, two aspirin, and get the hell out of here."

He dropped off the eggs and aspirin and gave me a smug smile. It was a smirk that said *it's about time you fucked up.*

"Thanks for saving my ass," I added.

"No problem, are you all right?" Guy props himself up on the metal bench that he uses as his confessional.

Rather than dodge him, I tell him the truth. "No, I'm not all right. As a matter of fact, I'm hurting. But I'll sober up— you'll be ugly the rest of your life."

He cracks up because he knows in male lingo it's my way of saying everything will be fine.

As Guy trudges off two hours late, I thank him again without the attitude. I think to myself how lucky I am to have people that take care of me when I'm in a jam.

Finally the kitchen is mine. Although I want to crawl up and take a nap on the pastry bench, the Bee would never allow me that luxury. From the moment it opens until the lights go off, there's a hum of energy, like a community within a community. Most days I fit right into that spiral, but today I'm thankful for a three o'clock lull. It gives me time to pick up a pen and one of my blank white index cards that I use for organizing by business.

Armageddon List
#1 Sell Business—call business brokers—ads in paper
    —call lawyer and accountant
#2 Get Motorcycle—Leathers
#3 Deal with Emily— finances? Job? Relationship?—
    slowly fade away
#4 Newspaper Column—Leave of absence
#5 Talk to kids—good luck and adios

I take the card and slip it into my pocket, because I will need a constant reminder. I want to get everything done before my self-imposed deadline of mid-June, coinciding with Bike week at Laconia.

As my hell day draws to a conclusion, I start to get my legs back under me. I also remember that I'll be going home to one pissed-off wife. I figure the best swerve to this impending head-on collision is to give her a call to restore the peace while it lasts.

I pick up the phone twice, dial half the numbers, and hang up both times. I'm looking forward to this little chat like a prostate exam. Regrettably, the third times a charm and thanks to caller ID, I get an icy greeting.

"So how was your day at work? You a little hungover?"

"No," I reply. "Very hungover."

"I thought you told me you were coming home at a decent hour, I was up half the night waiting for you."

"Look, I got a little drunk with my friends. Rather than drive totally sauced, I figured I'd sleep it off like a good citizen."

"And who were you sleeping it off with? An old girlfriend?"

"Only in my dreams. How was Professor Perfect?" As the words leave my lips, I realize that I should have written up this conversation on an index card beforehand. This was not going as planned.

"So are we planning on coming home tonight?" she asks.

"Yeah, I'm coming home. Sorry I fucked up last night."

"Bring your own supper home and remember to shut off the lights."

The conversation ends with a real healing touch.

"Okay."

As I finally push the last customer out the door, I realize I made a lot of headway. The checklist is complete, Emily's in the mood, and I survived until cocktail hour.

Feeling totally whipped, I was actually happy to be home. Happiness, however, was short-lived when I saw a nasty note on the table. It read, "Gone up to bed with Caesar. Do not disturb, favorite pillow and clothes are in the guest bedroom."

I don't mind being exiled to the second bedroom but what I can't stand is that little dwarf, Caesar, being anywhere close to my territory. When she bought that freak of a dog, there was only one rule we agreed to: I stay out of Caesar's food bowl, and Caesar stays out of my goddamned bedroom. I should be pleased with this development. Emily has followed my lead and lobbed some fresh artillery into our spat.

It's been years since I've slept alone, but I better start getting used to it if I want to execute my plan.

Step 1: Make my cave comfortable. I don't need a lot of trinkets or toys, just necessities. I've got to have a clock radio. It wakes me up, it talks to me in the middle of the night, and if it screeches at me in the morning, I give it a good slap. Being an avid reader and writer, there must be a good reading lamp, but the only one available is in my barn. It has a base of three clowns and a multi-colored lampshade. It gives the otherwise stately room a nice carnival atmosphere. I also grab my notebook that I use to write my columns and a stack of important periodicals to expand my mind. Like any knuckle-dragger, I have my favorites. *Vanity Fair* is not one of them. I need to be inspired by magazines such as *Easy Rider*, a motorcycle monthly with as much tits as chrome. Every boy should also have *National Geographic*. And to round off my reading list, I bring out my prized collection of *Naughty Neighbors* skin books. While other magazines have a lot more gloss and skin, nothing beats the down home talent that adorns the pages of this low-end porn mag. While most women are disgusted by pornography, I've always looked at it as fun and freaky. Like most men, I keep my porn safely tucked away in case the neighbors come over for high tea.

Deciding on one last jab before I hit the hay, I leave my July issue, with a frolicking farm girl on the cover, lying on the coffee table. I figure it'll be good reading for Emily if she gets lonely.

Before I know it, it is four A.M. and time to get back to work. Hitting the ground running, I go right to number one on my memo card that is now etched on my subconscious. I put together a list of people who might help me sell my business. It includes business brokers, people I trust in the industry, newspapers, and my ex-partner, Carl. He is in real estate and has a good working knowledge of my business. He has also sold other businesses before. I trust Carl, one of the few people I do. I also throw my accountant and lawyer on my growing list of people that need to know. The last person I put on the list is Emily. She will be the last person I tell, so that I don't stutter-step to my goal.

To get the ball rolling and try to remain functional at work, I give Carl a call. I ask him if he could stop down and chitchat. He asks what about. I tell him I'm thinking about selling the Bee. He's a little shocked but intrigued. Even though he's not an owner anymore, he still feels a part of his old business. He agrees to come down later that afternoon, because he knows that the place is a nuthouse on Saturdays.

The day slips by quickly. I haven't heard from Emily; she must be enjoying her magazine. Around four, I see a familiar face enter the back door. I haven't seen Carl in about six months but he never changes. He's friendly, focused, and in a lot of ways as disturbed as I am. As partnerships go, we had a good one. Fights were few. We faced our problems together and in the end we didn't have a messy divorce.

"Ian, I'm shocked," Carl said quietly. "I thought you were doing well. Why do you want to sell the Honey Bee?"

"Things are going well. Business is good, money's okay. I just know in my heart that it's time. I've been here close to ten years and I'm becoming stale."

"This catches me by surprise. Hell, I thought you'd be here forever."

"I feel like I have been."

"Do you have any idea what you might be asking for a price?" Carl wondered.

"Two million would be nice but realistically I'm probably looking at about 150K. I need half of the money up front, the rest I'd finance if the buyer is not a dubba. You know this would be the perfect family business. Mom, Dad, and all the children can work their balls off twenty-four hours a day. What would you be looking for a commission, Carl?"

I see his mind adding up figures, quickly. He was always a numbers guy. "I'd like five percent."

I counter with, "How's five grand? I'll give you the exclusive for two months and I'll buy all the advertising. The way the stock market is performing, maybe one of those laid-off high tech guys would like to be closer to the family."

"Two months doesn't give us much time," observed Carl.

"I know, but my plans are to take the summer off. I'd like to do a little writing and riding."

"How does Emily feel about this?"

I'd like to give Carl the bob and weave but I can't. He probably instinctively knows that there's something more going on. "I haven't told her yet. It's not like we haven't discussed it in the past, so I figure I'd do a lot of the leg work before I broach the subject with her."

I can see Carl looking uncomfortable, so I add, "If it makes you feel better, I'll talk to her tonight. But remember, this is my business, she has her own thing going on."

"It sounds like the wind is blowing from the north at the Payne ranch."

"Damn straight it is. So do we have a deal?"

"Yes."

After a cup of coffee and a hot apple turnover, Carl gets ready to head out, still inquisitive about what's really happening.

I tell him, "If you bring me some hot prospects, then I'll let you know what's going on. Otherwise, you'll have to wait for the book."

"Fair enough," he says. "I'll give you a call in the next couple of days and we'll get together."

As I wrap up another day, it feels good to accomplish so much. By dealing with someone I know on the deal, I've made my job a lot easier. I've come one step closer to crossing off something from my memo card.

My accomplishments leave me hungry so I grab a pound and a half of rib-eye from the cooler and head home for a good night of grilling and dreaming.

The flame of the grill and the moon are all the light I need to cook. With all that has been going on, food has been an afterthought. The smoke of the Weber slowly permeates the vicinity with the pungent odor of steak and garlic butter that I use for basting. Instead of attracting a friendly neighbor or hungry pooch, I hear the familiar click of the back door. This means Emily is on the way. As focused as I am on my plans, the fear of losing Emily still haunts me. It took me years to find her. We've been together ten years and I'll always love her. So maybe now it's time to give her some truth.

She rounds the corner to the backyard, her beautiful silhouette outlined by a single street lamp.

"How can you grill in the dark?"

"It's not that hard, the smell of the steak guides me."

"When you're done with your dinner, can we talk?" she asks.

"Sure. It will just take a minute."

Emily heads back in the house. I quickly take off the steak prematurely to think for a couple more minutes. The smoke stops rising from the grill and time has run out. Tonight I must face both Emily and myself.

Back in the house I devour my blood red beef. Emily is busy writing in the other room, which gives me the opportunity to taunt Caesar with a piece of meat that he will never get. Hearing the shuffle of papers alerts me that Emily is done.

"Ian, are you ready to talk?"

"Sure. About what?"

"Let's start with the other night and your card game. Then you also need to know that I got the Assistant Professorship and made my reservations for the seminar in June."

Emily's rapid-fire talk leaves me confused about where to begin. I decide to take the safe route.

"I'm so happy about the job. You've worked so long and hard and you deserve it. I knew you were going to the seminar when you first mentioned it at the Black Cow." While I offer my congratulations I can't help but think that the Professor has already slid into my Emily. I feel the rush of heat around my face, trying to hold in the rage toward her secret suitor. My plan is working perfectly.

"What happened Thursday night? You said you were coming home early. You didn't call. I was up all night worrying about you."

"This was the first time I've been home in a long time and maybe I got caught up in some unfinished history."

"It's your unfinished history that has always bothered me."

"It used to bother me, too. But going back home this time made me realize I can't fix every mess that I create. Sometimes they are just better left alone."

Before we get into our next volley, we give each other that thirty-second stare. I always look at her eyes to see if our conversation has been effective. Her expression will either say, "Okay, you're forgiven, let's go to bed" or "you disgust me, you came from under a rock." Today her eyes tell me the latter. I just wait, preparing myself for her lecture.

"Whatever your issues are," she starts, "you should have the damn common sense not to be driving around in the middle of the night, half-stewed. You have a lot of responsibilities. You're not a little kid, anymore. Besides, did you forget your own goddamned phone number?"

"Hey, I made it home in one piece. And why would I call anyway? I figured you were busy enough with the Professor."

I see Emily's eyes dip before she becomes a little flustered. Apparently, I have touched a sore spot. "This is the end of the conversation, I'm not talking to you when you're like this."

"No, actually I'm in a talking mood tonight," I say sarcastically. "I think our conversation should continue. You might be interested to hear some more news. I'm selling the Honey Bee."

She gives me a look of horror and then spits out, "Oh, that's just wonderful." She storms up the stairs with Caesar tagging along at her heels.

As irritated as I am, I think the conversation went well. In one day I have started to sell my business, had a meaningful conversation with Emily, took a jab at the Professor, had a great steak, and that little bastard Caesar didn't get any of it.

However, there is no time to dwell on my accomplishments for tomorrow is my donut day. I leap out of bed at two A.M. to hustle to the Bee to make donuts so that Guy can have a night off. As much as I detest getting up at that ungodly hour, it's always given me a little quiet time at the Honey Bee. I'm allowed to crank up some blues, glaze crullers, and daydream in peace.

This morning is different. I feel about as peaceful as the Gaza Strip. I can't get Emily out of my mind. As jealous as I claim not to be, I can only imagine the Professor seducing Emily with his long, soulful conversations. He can't be fucking sincere. As much as I'd like to pummel the egghead, he's a major part of my plans in detaching from Emily. I guess the real question is, why would I ever want to leave her? Before Emily, I had no direction. I could never follow through on anything.

As I fill the last donut and get ready to open the door to another day, I realize that the answer doesn't lie with Emily or the Professor. My frustration is not their fault. So as the first customers take their assigned seats, I get my first cup of joe and park myself behind the grill. After my quiet hours of denial, I now know that the answer lies only in the mirror.

As the sun peeks through the back door, orders start to pile up and I'm now in my Honey Bee zone. While other people need Prozac and Xanax to get away from their problems, all I need is the chaos of the Bee.

From seven to two, it is the usual Sunday, Elvis omelets, steak and eggs, and our world-famous Eat it and Beat it Breakfasts. The guest checks have no table numbers, just the first names of the customers. There's no need to write anything else. If it's Jimmy, it's two over with raisin toast. Phil's is three dropped on dry wheat. Grumpy's is three dropped in a bowl, well-drained, two orders of bacon crisp, and four butter patties. As monotonous as this routine might seem, it brings order to my madness.

Generally, by 2:30 we have fed everyone in town. It's also my twelfth hour when I usually start to run out of gas. Today, a phone call perks me up.

"Good afternoon, Honey Bee."

"Could I please speak with Ian Payne?"

Playing my own secretary I suspiciously ask, "Who may I say is calling?"

"This is Al from Seacoast Harley Davidson."

"Oh, in that case, this is Ian."

"Well, your bike's all prepped and ready to go. Would you like us to deliver it or would you like to come down and get it?"

"I'd prefer to pick it up. I'll shoot for a week from Wednesday afternoon, as long as everything is smooth at work."

"Sounds good. We're open until six P.M. on Wednesday."

"See you then." My normal grimace is replaced by my oral-sex smile.

Now all I can think of are the things that have to be done before I bring my baby home in a few days. It's only April and if I'm going to drive this bad boy home, I'm going to need some leathers. I regrettably confess that the leathers from my last trip no longer fit my manly body.

It's funny how that simple phone call relieved all of the pressures that have been chasing me lately.

THE NEXT WEEK flies by but not without the usual crises. The following Monday I was in bright and early, writing checks, checking my orders, and trying to get things tied up for my early exit on Wednesday.

Out of the blue, one of my waitresses came out back with a napkin dispenser. She was in a panic. A customer had complained of a white, powdery substance when they pulled out a napkin. Since we're a donut shop, this didn't alarm me. However, the local fire chief viewed the situation quite differently. He jumped into action, securing the mysterious napkin holder, fearful that it was laced with Anthrax. The local police were called to confiscate the suspect napkin holder and it was whisked off to the state capital for testing. I totally lost my mind, calling our local John Ashcroft every name in the book. He kept reminding me that he was just doing his duty. I continued to try to make him see the connection between a donut shop and a powdery, white substance but to no avail.

Although at first I was pissed off, I soon realized that this was an opportunity. My part-time job as a local columnist is my artistic release. But between running a business and my deadline at the newspaper, sometimes articles are hard to come by. I needed an easy column this week too, so it wouldn't interrupt my bonding with my black beauty.

Thanks to the local fire chief, this was the easiest column I ever wrote. I thought that even my feisty boss at the newspaper would love this one. Each column I submit is always under her watchful eye and verbal thrashing. If it's not bad English, it's my tendency to wander. Our loud battles have become legendary at the newspaper office. The more we yell and swear, the more we respect one another. Electra gave me the opportunity to write, I give her a new perspective with each new column.

As I stand at the grill, the column is already written in my mind and burning a hole in my head. But the mundane duties of the Bee keep me from putting pen to paper. That is until Casey walks through the door to see her mother, Annie, who was waitressing. Casey has worked for me since she was a junior in high school. Now she is an English major at the University of New Hampshire. She can also never say no. With her help, we bang out the column in no time. As I flip burgers and recite the day's events, Casey acts as my personal stenographer. Within an hour, the column is all wrapped up and ready for the paper.

That night I drop it off at Electra's and beg her not to change a word. It was sheer perfection.

Donut, Joe, and Cipro

The anthrax scare never really bothered me. I didn't inspect my letters or avoid government buildings. I must have been lulled into a false sense of security. I was wrong. Not only should we be on alert, we should all become John Ashcroft's junior G-Men. Attorney General Ashcroft has used his bully pulpit to ask us to be vigilant. Eyeballing everything from foreign-speaking folks to our neighbor's trash, all in the name of patriotism. There's a big difference between a good citizen and being Captain Queeg looking for the strawberries. My recent experience in bioterror borders on the bizarre.

Being the owner of a small donut shop breakfast joint I get to see it all. Vagabonds and working stiffs. Some are nice and some are a chore. My day always starts the same, bake the muffins and burn the homefries. However, this morning was interrupted by the local fire chief who decided this was the day to take over the soul of Barney Fife. Sheriff Andy was out of town and Deputy Fife had all the bullets in his gun. The incident started with a customer yanking a napkin out of a diner-style napkin dispenser. As she pulled it out a mysterious powdery substance came with it. The waitress, being informed of this, made the proper adjustments, dumping the napkins from the dispenser then cleaning and re-stocking it. Normally an incident of this type would pass without notice in our little donut shop but the eagle-eyed fire chief was quick to realize that the powdery substance could be a terrorist threat.

He immediately swept into action. He inspected the trash where the napkins were discarded. He interviewed the patrons who were obviously international targets. He immediately brought the unsuspecting patrons to the back sink to take a bleach bath to protect them from any residue from the mysterious powder. His next move, after infuriating the customers was to call the state capital to inform the hazardous material lab that the dangerous napkin dispenser would be secured and enroute within the hour. He informed me of his actions by phone at which time my Motorola became a tomahawk cruise missile. A few minutes later our eager civil servant was at the door snapping on his protective gloves to remove the dangerous cargo to a police cruiser for its trip to the State Lab. Before he could abscond with the napkin holder in question I mentioned that " this is a donut shop, there are a lot of powdery substances. Before you send this off to the guys in white suits could you try to connect the dots between a powdery substance and a donut shop?" Our local Jack Webb was not impressed by my attempt at sanity. He responded "Better safe than sorry." I replied, "At the cost of looking like a fool?" The conversation took a turn for the worse. Between a chorus of expletives deleted, I realized I was dealing with a fire chief who resembled Billy Bob Thornton looking for a merit badge. As he left with his booty he mentioned he was "just doing his job." And a helluva job it was.

The attentive officer wrapped the mysterious napkin holder in a plastic bag marked "evidence" and immediately whisked it off to the state capital. I was so mad I was levitating. My poor help had to listen to me rant and rave for the entire day. The alert waitress, Annie, will now be forever known as Annie-thrax. I will now call the police department on a daily basis to try and get the test results. Should I be gobbling up Cipro with my nightly Budweiser? Should I be looking for suspicious foreigners sitting in the corner table? Maybe I should just stick by my original thought and promote my soon-to-be famous Anthrax breakfast special: triple thick french toast loaded with powdered sugar. It's funny, I haven't seen Mr. Fife back in for his morning cup. Maybe he's getting his breakfast somewhere else. It's always the same—donut , joe, and Cipro to go.

The next morning Electra called and said, "You're article's great but it's a little short."

"You're a pain in the ass," I respond. "It might be a little short but it's the best article I've ever written."

"Did this really happen?"

"Every bleepin' word," I assure her.

"Okay, we'll be running it Thursday."

With the article out of the way, I can concentrate on more important matters. Going through the yellow pages, I notice an ad for custom leathers. The name of the business is Art's Cow Parts. The proprietor, cleverly enough, is named Art. I give him a call to see if he can meet my special requirements. In his own, unique way he brags that he can fit anyone into his leathers, from Pamela Anderson to Marlon Brando.

"Well, you should have no problem fitting a forty-ish, well-sculpted Adonis like myself, then."

"Sure, we fit all sorts of middle-aged fat guys."

I immediately bonded with Art. When I went to meet him the next morning, I wasn't disappointed.

Art stands about six foot four inches with a lanky frame. He's probably fifty-something. He has a cocky smile and a face that reads like a road map. He is also a true rebel. He served time in Nam, loves fast bikes, old cars, and young women. He likes politics, but hates politicians.

Art is also a master at his craft. I brought him my old leathers and told him that they brought me across country. I was hoping he could reproduce my good luck charms. While most people might find my superstitions juvenile, Art understood.

In the course of one hour, I had a great new set of leathers and I had made a connection with someone whose life seemed strangely parallel to mine. Each time we learned something about one another, it was like looking in a mirror. Our bad marriages were similar, we both ended up being Mr. Moms. We were both fiercely independent businessmen. I wrote for a newspaper, so did Art. I was stunned that I had found someone who thinks like me. I had previously thought that I was alone in the universe.

I RACE BACK to work to get everything ready for my day off. Luckily the weather was pretty good for early April. The anticipation of getting the motorcycle has me off my game.

By the time I leave, I have no clue if my work is done or not. All that keeps going through my mind is tasting the rarefied air of freedom the road gives you.

Back home, it is like preparing for a date with a sexy woman. The cologne of the fresh leathers is intoxicating. Putting on chaps is awkward at first but gives you a cowboy look. I scramble to beat dusk, when the temperatures drop to the low forties. I want a good initial ride to shake out the cobwebs of bikeless years.

Before I go, the whole package must be checked out. Male vanity is the worst kind—we look only at what we care to. If our gut is hanging over our belt, then we look at our shoes. The mirror does not lie.

The young man I feel like looks more middle-aged. The long, curly hair I used to have is now reduced to a barren waste-land of gray stubble. My brown, piercing eyes have not changed. They can be deep and soulful one moment and distant and deceiving the next. They are my best asset.

The bottom half of my face is dominated by a long, grizzly goatee that surrounds a mouth that is in constant motion. It can be caring or caustic—either way it never stops. My ears are curiously uneven due to a spider bite when I was little. My shoulders are strong and wide, due to what they have carried for years: big boxes, big problems, and big secrets. The rest of my six foot frame is imposing, anchored by size 14 feet. I was blessed with powerful legs, the source of my energy. My once lean torso is now sculpted by Anheuser Busch. Physical labor, however, has kept me from needing an abdominizer.

Today, there is no time to dwell on flaws. The reflection I see is damn near perfect.

I leave Emily one of the Post-it notes that have now become our main communication device. This saves us from any direct contact.

As I am running out the door, I hear the familiar sound of Emily's yuppie-mobile turning the corner. For some reason, my cocky biker strut turns self-conscious. The look she gives me would have been the same if I was cross-dressing. Verbal contact is now impossible to avoid.

Getting out of the car she rolls her eyes and says, "Jesus, I didn't know the rodeo was in town."

"Fuck off, I'm going to pick up my bike."

"How are you going to get your car back, Mr. Smart Guy."

"To be honest with you, I didn't even think of that."

"Would you like a ride?"

My giddy mood turns pensive. Against my better judgment, I say, "Sure." I add, "Just give me one minute, I have to grab something." I run in the house and grab a gift that Art had given me for buying the leathers. It was a woman's biker T-shirt and I had Emily in mind when I picked it out. It was two sizes too tight, jet black and on the front it read "Sick Bitch Motorcycles" in white letters. I figure this token might break the tension of the ride over.

All was quiet for the first couple of miles until Emily inquired, "Are all of those leathers really necessary?"

"Most definitely. Number one, they protect me from the

elements. Number two, I look really good in them. Especially the chaps, they make my penis look larger."

"That would be a pleasant surprise."

Well, at least she hasn't lost her humor. After a good chuckle, she says, "If you don't mind me asking, how much are you paying for the bike?"

"Sixteen thousand dollars."

"Oh my fucking God. That's a lot of money for a goddamned toy."

"Well, I figure with all the money you're going to be making at your new job, you'll be more than glad to buy it for me. How's the job going anyway?"

"I don't start for another week and I won't be making that much money at first."

"Gee, can't the professor open up his purse?"

"What the hell is it with you and the Professor? You seem a little irritated about him."

"Hey, I always like it when some guy wants to screw my wife."

"What the hell are you talking about?"

I now am in full control over the situation. There's nothing I like better than knowing someone's secret and using it for my personal amusement.

"You know I've always had a sixth sense, especially when it comes to male motives," I say.

"You're just talking foolishness. He has no interest in me."

In my most sarcastic tone, I reply, "If you say so."

Although I let her sneak out of the conversation, her body language reveals her anxiety. Emily has a tell, like any bad liar, when she is in nervous mode. It is a little repetitive movement that loudly states, "I am fibbing!" She twirls her hair with her finger.

She is now twirling up a storm.

"By the way," I interrupt, "I bought you a little gift." I proudly hold up the T-shirt for her viewing.

"Are you kidding?"

"No, I figure you can wear it on the bike. Would you like to go for a ride this afternoon?"

"We'll see. That's if you make it home alive."

"I know it's been a while since I've owned one but it's just like screwing, once you've done it, you always remember how."

She banters, "You might remember how but are you any good at it?"

Assuming she's referring to sex and not the bike, I reply, "Just because I haven't had a ride lately doesn't mean I haven't been practicing."

As we pull into Seacoast Harley, we're both laughing for the first time in a long time. I thank her for the ride and she responds with a long dissertation on why I should wear a helmet at all times.

"I appreciate your concern but helmet laws suck. I'll see you at home later."

"Yeah, if you make it."

WALKING AWAY from the car, I had a big shit-eating grin on my face. I was about to pick up the motorcycle that I had dreamed of all these years. Also, Emily and I had talked without strangling each other. Walking into the showroom, I begin the painful process of paperwork and congratulations that await me. The insurance, the sticker, the ringing of the salesman's bell to indicate that some dumb fuck, namely me, is a proud new Harley owner.

After an eternity, I head to the rear of the building. The

salesman opens the door and the April sun is shining on my black beauty. For some people, this might be another toy added to their collection. For me, it is much more. This is my liberation day. My life will now change. The bike is only a small part of the puzzle, it's a tool that helps aid my freedom.

While all of these thoughts are rambling around in my head, the salesman is wrapping up his three-minute speech on the dipstick, headlights, and blinker. I don't listen to a word. There is no need for this information, the bike and I already bonded on that cold, winter day when I first saw her.

The salesman gives me a final few useless tips and then asks if there is anything else he can do. The answer is easy: just go away. He heeds my last request and I slowly drive out to US Route 1. Sitting at a stop sign, I notice the undeniable growl of my new ride. She is ready and so am I. We start off down the road. We'll test each other today. I will get to know her limits and she will get to know mine. It has been awhile since I have ridden. The smells of the road, the element of danger, the power and noise are all falling back into place. In less than an hour, our melding will be complete.

Heading toward home, I am frozen. Forty five degrees at fifty miles per hour equals popsicle even with leathers, chaps, and gloves. My body might be cold but my blood is pumping. The new ride and the taste of the road are like a drug.

Pulling into the driveway, Emily pokes her head out of the window. She tries her best to give me an "I'm embarrassed for you" look but my smile caught her off guard and she relaxed. She comes outside to view the new monster.

"Jesus, that's big."

Before she can utter another word, I respond, "You never complained before. Do you want a ride? We'll just go around the block."

Skeptically, she says, "Isn't it too cold?"

"No! Besides, I'll warm you up afterward."

She grins as she goes into the house to bundle herself up. I can't help but grin myself. Apparently the new heartthrob is slow on the draw. The banter Emily and I exchanged today could only make me conclude that the Professor needs a refresher course on getting laid. Maybe he's all talk and no cock.

As Em bounces down the stairs I put my thoughts on the back burner and enjoy having a beautiful woman on the back of my bike. We tool around town for a couple of quick laps before the sun goes down. As cold as it is, it's nice to feel Emily's arms around me. I savor these moments because while our love is still evident, our lives and interests are racing off in different directions.

After our ride, I nestle my baby into her bay in the barn and head into the house to thaw myself out and hopefully Emily, as well.

As I TRUDGE into the house, I mentally prepare for World War III. Surprisingly enough, Emily is sparking up a fire.

"You must be frozen, I'm as cold as ice and I was only out there for half an hour," she says.

Rather than make some snide remark, I reply, "Yeah, I'm cold as hell. The fire will feel great. I'm going to pour myself a glass of Crown Royal. Would you like one?"

"Maybe in a bit, I've got some papers left to grade."

"How long do you think it'll take you?"

"Why?" she asks suspiciously.

"I thought I could maybe take you out to dinner."

"Why?"

"Maybe you're hungry, maybe we could have a long, soulful conversation, or maybe I should just cut to the chase and ply you with liquor and screw your brains out."

"Well, I am hungry."

She heads off to her office with that little prick Caesar following her. I sit by the fire and suck up my Crown Royal, thinking that victory is at hand. I am so fucking content that I take a trip to la-la land. I wake up a half-hour later with Crown Royal poured all over my lap. I'd feel like a loser but it is the first time I've had a nap in twenty years.

I stumble off to the shower to get dolled up for my date. Getting dressed, I realize that I am starting to slowly morph into a biker on a full-time basis. Rather than khakis and tie shoes, it's now jeans and my biker boots. My black turtleneck is now accessorized with a leather vest. My goatee has seemed to grow overnight. It now reaches to the top of my chest.

As I head back to the fire, I grab a pen and paper. I might have time to start working on my next article. Before I have a chance to start, Emily finishes her work and heads for the shower. On her way she stops and gives me an eyebrow.

"Jesus, where are you taking me? Wally's?" Wally's is one of the most notorious biker bars in New England.

"Sounds good. Why don't you dress up in your new titty-tight Sick Bitch T-shirt and we'll head over for a couple of pitchers and a pizza."

"Sounds delightful," she says as she heads off to the shower.

I turn back to my writing and think of what a kick it would be to see Emily all decked out in biker gear, as opposed to her usual muted earth tones.

I quickly fade back to the dream world of my latest story called "Vatican Vacation." There's nothing that makes me happier than some good Catholic bashing, especially when it's about horny priests, pedophiles, and a Cardinal who sleeps with all of them.

I soon hear an unfamiliar click descending the stairs. As

Emily turns the corner, I'm shocked to find her in full biker bitch regalia, black boots with fuck-me heels, peel off jeans, her new skintight top, and a black vest.

"You look fucking beautiful."

"Enough Crown Royal and you'll say anything."

"Hey, I'm not lying, I can hardly stand up."

"Tie it down, cowboy, I'm hungry."

Now all I can think is don't fuck this up. Don't open your big mouth. Rather than take the chance of a long drive over to Wally's, I suggest a quick jaunt over to Rick's, a local watering hole a half-mile down the road. This is the perfect spot, it has enough noise to minimize conversation.

When we get there, I'm in for another surprise. Rather than hide out in the corner, which is her usual M.O., Emily suggests we go belly-up to the bar. I now need to pinch myself. This is too good to be true. I think to myself that there must be a catch but it just kept getting better.

Before she excuses herself to the bathroom, rather than order her usual cabernet, she asks for a B-52. I order my usual shot and a beer and ask John, the bartender, if he would do Emily a double.

John asks, "Are you guys celebrating?"

"I'm trying and a double will help."

John gives me that simple nod of the head that signifies his male understanding.

Emily struts back to her stool and I can't help but notice the losers at the bar, inspecting her ample rack.

"Hey hun, I'm not the only one admiring you tonight."

"What do you mean?"

"Half the bar was sniffing you out on the way back."

"So this is what you guys like." She smirks and throws back her B-52.

We order another round and she starts to change the subject.

"So what's going on with the Honey Bee," she inquires. "Are you really serious about selling?"

"Yeah, I think the timing is right. And I'm getting stale."

"How much are you going to ask for it?"

"I want 150 grand. I'll take some paper but I'd like most of the money up front."

"How are you going to sell it?"

"Carl's going to market it for me and act as the business broker for a set fee."

"What are you planning on doing if it sells?"

"I'm taking the summer off. In my whole life, I don't think I've had a whole fucking week off. I'll figure out what I'm going to do later. First, I'm heading up to Bike Week in Laconia."

"When's Bike Week?"

"It's the third week of June."

"I'll be at my conference the third week of June. Besides, with the new job, it's going to be a busy summer for me."

"I realize that. But remember, I haven't sold the Honey Bee yet."

"No, but it seems like you have your ducks all in a row."

"Yeah, but it's nice to dream in real time."

The conversation slowed as Emily finished her third B-52. I better start to move before she's knee-walking.

"Can I ask you a question? Are you getting tired of sleeping with Caesar?"

"One dog is as good as another."

"If that's true then can we throw Caesar out tonight?"

"Sure," she says. The liquor has obviously taken effect.

Before the mood changes, we head out for a short drive home. When we get inside the house there are no words exchanged, only a short stare. We start to kiss each other in the living room, like two kids in high school locked in an insepa-rable hug, knowing at any time it could end. In that moment, without talking, we know instinctively that our lives were slowly pulling in different directions for different reasons. My reasons were complex. I felt like my life was suddenly on the down side and it wasn't just my age. All the dreams I once had were now on the clock. Death and the frailty of my life were starting to chase my subconscious.

Both my sisters died too young. Now I am the same age they were when their lives ended. Maybe if I had been able to say goodbye I would feel more in control of my fate. But the terms under which they passed away weren't in anyone's con-trol. Katherine was shot by her third husband while Carol was drowned in a riptide called life. Neither survived long enough to know how much they meant to people. Would my life mir-ror theirs? Could I be next?

While all of these thoughts quietly grind through my mind, I notice that Emily is holding on as tight as I am. What is her fear? Could her emotional lovemaking with the Professor be her salvation or her torment? I never could read her mind and I was always scared to ask. For any guy there is always the un-derlying fear of being too close.

As we head off to bed our lovemaking seems to reflect both of our souls. Hers might be growing and blossoming. Mine is just fighting to hang on. Tonight, our sex is as volatile as our spirits. Our normal lovemaking is passionate but restrained. Tonight, the shackles are off because fear is ruling our world.

Afterwards, we both quietly fall into a coma. It hadn't been that long that we slept apart, but having my beautiful Emily back next to me was the ultimate sleeping pill.

Morning came too quickly. Em had to work. She had that soft morning look that a woman gets when she first wakes up.

She asked me what I was going to do. I told her that the motorcycle and I were going to do some heavy bonding. Emily wished me luck as we headed down to the kitchen for a coffee.

Before heading out the door, she turned and said, "Ian, I still love you. But I feel we're slipping away from each other. In a way, I might be as guilty as you."

I just sat there with my eyes open and my mouth shut. While she thought she was speaking in female, I knew exactly what was happening. She was telling me that her heart was on the move. And I was helping it along.

As EMILY PULLS out of the driveway, I quickly turn channels and my attention is now focused on my ride. For late April the weather was unseasonably warm. The temperature was already in the fifties and it was only nine in the morning. I could skip the chaps today.

I packed the saddlebag with all of the necessary ingredients. These include: riding gloves, shades, two cheap pens, a one by two foot-piece of bakery butcher paper (that all of my articles are written on), a pack of 'Boros, one joint, fifty bucks, and a Balpin hammer. While the hammer might seem out of place, it comes in very handy when some asshole decides to drive you off the road. You simply pull up next to them at a stoplight and bust out his fucking taillight. If no stoplight is available, the hammer can be used as a perfect projectile that can find its way through a back window. The hammer can be explained away to the local Joe Friday as an auto body tool rather than an implement of destruction. Besides, it's much less conspicuous than a 9 mm or a k-bar.

All loaded up, I roar out of the driveway heading toward the coast. Starting at Seabrook beach, I weave my way up the shoreline. I soon pass through Hampton Beach and see the first sign of summer, workman's trucks at all of the little shanties and businesses, getting ready for the onslaught of the tourist season.

This beach holds special memories for me. I owned a business here for one season of hell. The only people who make money at these summer resorts are the landlords. They squeeze every fucking penny out of the businesses that occupy their rat holes. The only other profitable enterprise is drug dealing, which is bustling all summer.

My particular business was called Big Daddy's, home to French bread pizza and coconut cruises, a virgin pina colada that was served in a fresh coconut. After the first month, I knew I was losing my shirt so I put three fingers of rum in the cruisers, for an extra three bucks. While this was highly illegal, it ended up being the second most lucrative thing that I sold. My number one profit maker was advice. For one dollar, you could ask Big Daddy any question. During that summer, people asked me 2,500 questions. I kept all of the advice money up in a panel in the ceiling. When I left after labor day it was all I had left of my dream of franchising Big Daddy's.

This is the first time I've returned since that summer ten years ago. Big Daddy's is now a Subway. The beach is still littered with T-shirt shops, arcades, and fried dough joints. The center piece of the beach is the Casino, the summertime home to musical has-beens like the Monkeys, Grand Funk Railroad, and, God forbid, Eddie Money. As much as the music sucks, the building is equally as dilapidated, prime for one of those mysterious winter fires that occur after a bad season.

As I drive out of Hampton, the only good memory that I can think of is the T & A that strutted up and down the boardwalk on hot summer days.

Heading north up Route 1A, the road snakes its way through miles of beautiful seascapes on one side and ostentatious mansions on the other. This is New Hampshire's Gold Coast. While it's less than twenty miles long, the majority of wealth in the state is concentrated here.

With wealth comes privilege and with privilege comes obnoxious bastards. I make a particular point to ride extra hard and loud in these areas to disturb their daily bridge games and croquet matches. Rye is the richest of these communities. It's a town where everything is just swell, including the swelled heads of all of the residents. Before I leave Rye, I have to take a break at one of their many scenic vistas that overlook the Atlantic. This is the perfect place for a good smoke. What makes it especially pleasing is the disdain that the local walkers convey as I foul their rarefied air. As I leave Rye, I always feel obligated to leave a memento. A cigarette butt will do.

My favorite town on the coast is Portsmouth, an old sea town littered with good saloons, upscale shops, and the best looking women in New Hampshire. They're rich enough to look good but poor enough to still want to get laid. In the warm weather, my favorite perch is a string of outdoor decks down on the waterfront. The first deck is a prime location. It has the best view of the busiest corner of Market Street where there is a constant parade of tramps and tarts.

My articles always have a good flow when I'm writing on the docks. The beer always tastes better, it could be the sea air. On a sunny spring day, this is heaven. Two beers and a hundred glances later, my story is done a week ahead of time.

I decide to continue my ride but first I need to stop and check out another dream I hope to realize. I walk up a small set of stairs and enter Hobo's Tattoo. As I'm browsing through the giant board of designs, one of the artists comes out from his working cocoon and asks if he can help. His name is Jason and he has been working at his craft for ten years. He started in his mother's house in Worcester tattooing his friends and has been working his art ever since. While our conversation only lasts a short time, I know that Jason will be the one to tattoo me. Jason is intrigued by my plan to tell my life story on my body in hieroglyphics.

The idea indirectly came from Emily. While she studied for her Masters in Archaeology, I kept peeking at all of her books on hieroglyphics. I became fascinated by the symbols of the language of the ancients. The tribal forms of the writing would seemingly make great tattoos. Now that the Professor has targeted Emily, I have another reason to adorn my body with hieroglyphs.

The room starts to fill up with well-tattooed patrons and Jason has to get back to work. Before leaving, I promise Jason that I'll be back with my story and the symbols so I can be his human canvas.

It's barely noon but I feel like I've accomplished so much today. I don't know if it is enthusiasm or the powerful drug of freedom.

THE REST OF MY day off is spent making love to the road. From Portsmouth I head up I-95 to see how the new motorcycle handles on the highway. While the temperature is nearing sixty, at seventy mph it feels like I am freezing my balls off. About one hour is all I can take without putting on the chaps.

I take the Old Orchard Beach exit and pay homage to the small French vacation spot. It's crammed with little honkytonks, a beautiful boardwalk, and seven miles of pristine beach. I pull my bike up to my favorite spot. JB's is a shot and a beer bar that overlooks the nearby amusement park. In the summer it is populated with scantily clad French girls, bikers, and local troublemakers. It is one of the few places left where there is always a good fight, but nobody ever takes it seriously. JB's was a hotspot even when I was a kid. I used to be across the street trying to fool the guesser, an old Greek man who made a living at telling you your weight, height, or occupation for one dollar. If he guessed wrong, he would give you a valuable prize, like a plastic comb or a whistle ring. I remember he retired not long ago, headed for Florida. There was a story in the newspaper about a week later. The IRS had seized his assets. Although he had fooled me, apparently he didn't have any luck with Uncle Sam.

By the time I finish my Bud, it is already two and time to head back. I take Route 1 down through Saco, Kennebunkport, and York to get back to Portsmouth. It is a great hour-and-a-half ride. I stop for a quick rest by the salt piles on the riverfront. As I get off the bike, I feel that buzz that I haven't felt for years. The combination of vibration, the smell of the road, and the exhilaration that you know you could be dead at any second give you a mild high when you've been on a bike for a good amount of time. This is the end to a perfect day.

I HATE FRIDAY morning. After a day off, no one should wake up that early in the morning. It sucks. The weather is grim today and I just don't feel like picking up where I left off. But no matter how hard I fight it, the Honey Bee sucks me right back into its hive. There is no time to think. The pieces must be picked up before the weekend.

When I come in everyone is quiet. That usually means there is something they don't want to tell me. Today seems deadly silent. When this happens, the first thing I usually do is check the refrigerators and major components to see if they are working. Everything seems in working order so I'm going to have to probe deeper. I do this through the chain of command. I am the worker bee; if I want to know what's going on I have to ask the Queen Bee. Regina opened this morning so I have to prime her for information.

"There was a little trouble in paradise yesterday. Your girl-friend, Rotha, slapped Casey in a fit of rage because she had to wait for her cappuccino," she informs me.

"You're shitting me. Did Casey kick the crap out of her?"

"You know Casey, she's too nice. She could never do anything like that. The customers and I took care of it. It was right when the shifts were changing. Casey was pretty upset though, you might want to give her a call."

"If that skankadroid Rotha dares come in here, do not serve her. I want to deal with her myself. See, I won't mind slapping that bitch, it'll feel great."

I give Casey a quick call and assure her that that douche bag will never be seen on my premises again.

I forgot that a good cat fight at the Bee is great for business. And the two participants in this brawl are perfect. Casey is Rebecca of Sunnybrook Farm. No one ever has said a bad word about her. She has a great smile and couldn't hurt anyone if she tried.

Rotha is Cruella DeVille. No one likes her. She has a bad word for everyone, especially behind their back. She is the Evil Empire. This is the US against the Japs in WWII. Good and bad are easy to recognize. But even Rotha will have a defender or two. For now, all I have to do is sit and wait for the next bomb.

In Seabrook, like a lot of small clanny towns, people side with their own, even if it hurts. As the morning rolls on in between breakfast and baking, I listen to the customers from a small room connecting the kitchen and dining room. Today, the bays are buzzing and the consensus of opinion is that Rotha is the Devil. Even the few people that will sit next to her are trashing her. The trial and execution will be swift. In fact it will be over as soon as she shows up.

Although Fridays are usually hectic enough between deliveries, payroll, and the scramble to get things ready for the weekend, the slapping incident made everything even more chaotic. Whenever I'm extra stressed, I immediately take as many things off of my plate as I can. I focus only on the important and turn a blind eye on any bitch moan or groan.

This is the type of day where the phone rings nonstop. I don't know where they get my name but nine times out of ten it is some shithead in a cubicle. They want to sell me everything from light bulbs to ballpoint pens embossed with my business's name. The calls that piss me off the most are from police and fire benevolent associations, DARE programs, and any so-called good causes. They try to pull at your heartstrings by telling you your money will be going to help the less fortunate. The way I look at it, I'm the less fortunate. I never met a cop or fireman that didn't have a new four by four with all the extra trinkets. So usually I just tell them to screw off and then I just hang up the phone. But on a day like this I figure I'll just bust their balls.

"Hi, Ian, this is the Seacoast DARE program. We were hoping that you could help us out with an ad in this year's program. We really appreciated your help last year and we hope we can count on you again. A business card-sized ad is $100, a quarter page is $150, and a full page is only $200. It would really help the kids stay off drugs."

Before hanging up the phone I think, maybe it's time to help out the little drug addicts with a nice ad.

"I'll take a full page."

The con man gets all worked out and lets out a squeal like he's getting a BJ without having to pay. "Thanks, Ian, the kids are really going to appreciate it. What would you like your ad to read?"

"In big letters on the top of the page I want 'Honey Bee Donuts.' Below that, I want 'Smoke a joint — eat a donut — the perfect hive for your good buzz.'"

After a long pause, he says, "You're kidding, right?"

"No. You put the ad in and I'll pay for it." I have now accomplished my mission of wasting this prick's time and humoring myself. He abruptly hangs up the phone. I guess that means the ad won't be running this year.

I didn't even get to put down the phone and wipe the shit-eating grin off my face when the goddamned thing rings again. I answer it in my best leave-me-alone-tone. "Honey Bee."

"Hey Ian, this is Carl. Sounds like you're having a great day." He always was good at reading my moods. "I have a little news that might cheer you up."

Skeptical, I say, "Try me."

"Would it make your day if I told you that I found someone interested in the Honey Bee?"

"Jesus, that was fast."

"The best news is that he has money. I was thinking about taking him on a drive by the place this afternoon."

"That sounds good because Fridays are always busy."

"Do you have all of your paperwork in order?" Carl asks.

"No, but I'll have it by the first of the week - four year's tax returns and up-to-date sales."

"Could I bring him in mid-week?"

"Hell, if he's got money you can bring him in today."

Carl replaces my giddiness with anxiety. "You've got to clean the place up and make it look good, just like selling a car."

I give him my usual "no problem," knowing that it will be a monumental task to clean up the place in less than a week.

Carl says, "I'll give you a call at the first of the week then."

Setting down the phone, there is no time for even a smile.

The orders are all backed up and everybody's screaming for something. Quickly, I shift into my panic mode. This usually starts with a medium-loud "I hate this fucking place" and a swift toss of a spatula against the wall.

Even though no one wants to get near me, miraculously, they all know what to do. In crisis state, Cindy is the one to keep me organized. She not only knows what I need, but more importantly, she knows what I don't need. She can be my secretary one minute and my dishwasher the next. Cindy instinctively knows when to stop making turnovers and focus my aggression. Half an hour later, you'd never know we were busy. No matter how screwed up things are, or how hit and run my mood is, it changes so fast that my help never really notices.

When everything calms down, I think of all of the calls that I have to start making. First, I give my accountant, Vernon, a buzz and ask him for some fresh tax returns. Figuring I'm in trouble he asks me what's wrong. This is predictable because I keep him in the dark about everything that I can. He makes sure that I pay the Feds and the state, he does my payroll, and he balances my bank statements. Besides that, Vernon is my Sergeant Schultz, he knows nothing. I tell him that I may have someone interested in the Honey Bee.

He sounds surprised and asks, "When did this all come about?"

"I put it out about a month ago and I already got a nibble."

"I can bring the returns down to you tomorrow. If you don't mind me asking, what do you plan on doing if you sell?"

"My only plan is to take the summer off."

"Can you afford to do that?"

"You tell me, you're my accountant."

The conversation ends quickly because my secretive ways make it impossible for him to answer the question.

While I'm on a roll, I give my lawyer, Alan, a call. I give
him a run down on what's going on and ask him if he'd be willing to draw up the paperwork on the sale and keep me legal.
Alan reminds me that the Honey Bee is a landmark and asks if
I've thought about what kind of person I want to sell it to.

"One with money," I answer.

Alan says, "That's fine, but you better get enough up front
so you don't get dragged back. You have to be careful if you're
going to take any paper. The Honey Bee is the second home to
many of your customers and you work your balls off making
sure that it feels like theirs. Do you think somebody else would
be able to do that as well?"

"Alan, everybody is replaceable. It's not like I'm a fucking
brain surgeon, I'm a grill cook."

"You know that's bullshit," he says. "You might be good at
flipping eggs but there's a lot more that goes into what you do."

"I know, I'll keep my eyes open."

"What do you plan on doing if you sell?"

"I'm going to drive around on my motorcycle for the rest
of my life and write a fucking book."

Alan laughs and says, "Sure, we'd all like to do that. Just
give me a call when you're ready, and I wish you lots of luck."

"Thanks, Alan."

With all that's going on, the day is already winding down,
hundreds were fed, I pissed off the appropriate number of
people, and as we are closing in on May my checklist is already
starting to dwindle.

As the final employee is trudging out the door, I drag out
my little index card, my Armageddon list. It's frightening how
much progress has been made. Number one, to sell the business, is already in motion. Number two, to get the motorcycle,
is complete and I scratch it off my list. Number three is dealing

with Emily, on some days it feels like I'm in control of this situation, but on others I'm as lost as I've always been with her. Number four is leave of absence at the newspaper. I'll wait a little longer on this one. It's not like I'm writing for the fucking *Times*. Besides, it's the only job that I've ever really loved while getting paid. Number five is talk to the kids. It's been a while since we've touched base. Maybe this is the perfect time to give them a buzz.

I dial up my son's cell phone and get his usual message. It says something about returning your call but that never happens. The message I leave I put in my phony "urgent' voice, making it feel like someone got hit by a car. I'm assured that he'll call me back because Francis, my son, is as sensitive as I used to be. He is always busy chasing his dream in his chosen field of music, from being a DJ when he was a teenager to playing big clubs in Boston. He is now in his mid-twenties. Fran and his group, Universal Tongues, are getting ready for their EP release this summer. He's spending more and more time in New York and plans on moving there in the near future.

My daughter, Nicky, is a totally different story. She was the sharp one. You could never get anything by her and she always got her way. I admired her skillful manipulation of everybody and everything that stood in the path of what she wanted. She played me like a violin. Maybe it was a father-daughter thing but I could never say no to her. I poured all of my failures into making sure that she went to college. After two years at Northeastern, she wanted out in the worst way. It was the only time she ever demanded anything from me and didn't get her way. She stuck it out and got her accounting degree.

About two months before graduation, she called me up and told me there was someone that she would like me to meet. Emily and I had dinner with Nicky and her new beau, Sammy.

I hated this prick from square one, not because he was screwing the shit out of my daughter and not because he was a Puerto Rican homeboy from Brooklyn. I hated this little shit because he agreed with everything that I said that night at dinner. His vocabulary was limited to one word, "exactly." If I said to this dink, "You know, I'd really like to bomb Puerto Rico right off the fucking map," he'd nod approvingly and say, "exactly."

A month after our dinner, I got another call from my daughter. She asked me if I was sitting down. She might as well have been holding up a big flashing billboard that said, "I'm knocked up." I just shut up, however, and waited for her confession.

"Daddy, I don't want you to worry but I found out I am pregnant."

For once I decided not to open my big yap and just listen to her paint a rosy picture.

"Sammy and I are so happy. I know I'm just graduating school but I've never been more positive about anything in my life."

I hear Sammy in the background babbling about wishing he could tell me in person. But seeing how I felt about Sammy, this probably would not have been a good move for the creep. However, my daughter must have felt the love that I had for Sammy so she put him on the phone so that I could congratulate him.

No matter what I said to him about the responsibility to his child and my daughter, all he kept muttering was that word, "exactly," agreeing with everything I said. I was not alone in my distrust of Sammy. My son also hated his guts. As time went on, Sammy proved us right. He convinced my daughter that marriage might be in the future. The closer she got to delivery, the more he was screwing everything that walked. He kept his own apartment rather than move in with my daughter. This was helpful with knocking up his other girlfriend.

Rosie was born two years ago, Superbowl Sunday. As much as I wanted to kill Sammy, I went to the hospital trying to lend support to my daughter and to give him one last chance at stepping up. This was one of the few times that I didn't go with my first instinct which would have been to beat him within an inch of his life. Our conversation was short, it ended with his first "exactly." I knew from that point on that my daughter would have no husband, my granddaughter would have no father, and I would maintain a lifelong vendetta against that cocksucker Sammy.

Things soon began to quiet down with Nicky and we got into a routine: I'd see my granddaughter, Nicky would milk me for as much cash and goodies as she could. As I noticed the pattern escalating, I received another SOS. My daughter was on the phone bawling about being knocked up again by the same Puerto Rican puppy-machine. The joyous news made me so happy that I must have gone crazy. Due to the tactful nature of my conversation with my daughter that evening, it left us estranged for almost a year.

I missed the birth of my second granddaughter, Maya, but I wasn't the only one. The father of the year skipped out on it, too. I started to make up with Nicky under a new set of rules: no matter how many little bastards she had, I wasn't the fountain of money. Two other realizations have dawned on me since some time has passed. Number one, I always thought I was a pretty good father, I was wrong. Number two, the only person I will ever want to kill, by any means possible, for the rest of my painful existence, will be that scumbag and ex-future son-in-law, Sammy. Ordinarily I am not a violent human being but hearing the word "exactly" anywhere, anytime is now my trigger. Only somebody with no balls at all could agree with someone "exactly."

A couple days later I finally heard from my son.

"Hey Pop, what's up?"

"Hey Francois, how's it going?"

"Just working my ass off."

"What's happening with the EP?"

"We're just about finished," he tells me. "We've been spending a lot of time with vocalists fine-tuning the sound."

"Sounds good, homeboy. Just remember if you make your millions I want to be head of your posse so I can suck every last dime out of you."

"Thanks, Dad. You always were thinking about my best interests."

"Why I called the other day was to invite you and your sister out to dinner. I need to talk to you."

"Why, what's wrong?" Francis asks in a concerned tone.

"Nothing, it's just that things might be changing at work a bit and if they do I might be taking off for the summer."

"You're kidding, right?"

"No. I put the Bee up for sale and I got a strong nibble so if this happens I don't want to throw you guys any curve balls."

"When do you think this might happen?"

"You never know but the sucker's supposed to come look at it this week. I was thinking we could get together a week from Wednesday. Could you track down your sister for me? Christ, she never answers her phone. Just have her give me a call. Tell her I'll pay for a babysitter so we don't have to go to Chuck E. Cheese."

"All right. How's Emily taking all of this?"

"Pretty good, she started her new job so maybe I can mooch off her for a while."

"Yeah, in you dreams."

"Give me a call back after you hear from your sister. We'll shoot for a week from Wednesday. Love ya, kid."

"Love ya, Pop."

CARL CALLED ME on Monday and let me know that they'd be down on Wednesday morning. He informed me that his client's name was Dimitri Pouliopoulos, a thirty-something Greek immigrant with a big family and an uncle with some dough. I told Carl that everyone was busting their balls cleaning the place and it would be in good shape by Wednesday morning. Everybody was curious about the urgency to clean so I told them that the health Nazi was making the rounds.

Emily and I resumed our routine of sleeping apart. We didn't discuss it, we just knew we'd be better off this way for the time being. Besides, having started the new job, she'd be working late. I'm always in bed early and if she really needs me I'm right down the hall.

By Wednesday morning, the Honey Bee was spotless. It almost seemed creepy because everything was too organized. The Honey Bee is housed in a 1960s block building. It consists of 2,500 square feet, half of which is dining, the other half is kitchen. It seems everything is in the wrong spot, but for some strange reason it all seems to work perfectly.

The back room has a centerpiece of two oversized butcher block bakers' tables. There is a row of shelves suspended from the ceiling around the whole perimeter of the room. These are packed with every conceivable type of cup, napkin, container, coffee, and wholesale box known to man. Tucked under all of the shelving are a handful of refrigerators, a huge dough mixer the size of a small car, two convection ovens, a 3 x 3-foot donut fryolator, a donut glazer, and an oversized proof box. The grill is tucked in a twelve by eight-foot corner. It consists of a six-foot flat top, two burner stove, two toasters, and two microwaves. Eggs, plates, and breads fill every inch of the metal shelving that surrounds the grill. People that visit the back room of the Honey Bee always comment on how good everything smells. In some sense, it must bring them back to their childhood before everything came out of a cellophane package and tasted like cardboard. The back room of the Honey Bee never sleeps. Pastry is made all day, donuts are made all night, and breakfast is from six in the morning to six at night.

While the back room is known only to a few, the front is truly the Honey Bee. Personal treasures cover every inch of the walls. A colorful collage of hundreds of license plates, donated by the customers, clutters every nook and cranny. A picture of Teddy Roosevelt looms over the register like a watchful eye. There are antique photos of the Titanic, boxers, and wrestlers. There are model ships and airplanes. There is a variety of animal antlers. An oversized picture of the Statue of Liberty keeps tabs on bay two. On top of the Coke machine there is a five-foot model of the Capitol Building. Neon glows from the front windows. While there are only six tables and two horseshoe bays with ten stools each at any time of day it seems to house the whole community. The owner of the Honey Bee is the town of Seabrook. I am only the caretaker.

As CARL AND DIMITRI slip in through the back door, I can't help but wonder who this hairy-backed interloper coming to steal my creation is. I introduce myself with a half-hearted handshake. We hide over in the corner of the room so as not to be overheard by the help.

In a just-off-the-boat accent, Dimitri explains that Carl had already given him a lot of the info that he needed. For the past five years he had worked for his uncle in the pizza business and had now saved up enough money to buy a place of his own. He informed me that he would have his whole family to help him. His wife and nieces would be the waitresses and he would be head cook. He makes great pizza, baklava, and spinach pie. His brother, George, had just come over from Athens and would serve as the donut maker.

After our short but to the point conversation, I take Dimitri for a walk around the Bee. While he is impressed by all the people at the stools, I can see he isn't impressed by my choice of decor. He jokingly asks if I am running an auto salvage or a restaurant. I laugh along with Dimitri, but I really wanted to kick him right in his Greek balls.

All I can think of is Dimitri taking over the Honey Bee and replacing its character with the five shabby-framed pictures of Athens that adorn every Greek pizza shop on the East Coast. Hey, but if he buys it, it's no longer my business. What do I care as long as I get my money? I try to remember what my lawyer, Alan, said rather than letting my ego get in the way.

The tour only was quick because the Honey Bee isn't that big. We catch up with Carl in the back room where he's schmoozing with Rollie, the morning cook. Rollie had been at the Honey Bee for over nine years through heart attacks, operations, and cancer. You just can't get rid of this guy. I thought to myself, geez, after all these years if Dimitri and his band of pizza peddlers buy the place, Rollie will finally be going down. It just didn't seem right.

I gave Carl all of the paperwork that Dimitri had requested. He needed to go back and kiss up to his uncle before getting the OK to buy the Bee. There would also be some Greek bartering on my asking price. The phrase "How much? Too much" will now enter our negotiations.

Dimitri and Carl go out the back door and I walk them

out to his car. Dimitri's Mercedes probably cost fifty grand. My negotiating posture has changed as I bid them farewell. If the motherfucker can drive a Benz, he can afford the Honey Bee.

At the end of the day, Carl gave me a call and told me that the indications were that Dimitri was going to buy. He did ask Carl if there was any leeway on the price. Carl told him that he didn't think so but that I would be willing to take some paper.

I took an extra long time that night with my Bud and my 'Boro thinking about all of the things that would change if that Greek horde bought the Honey Bee. Who would Guy make donuts for? What about Regina and Helen, who have faithfully opened the doors all these years? Then there's Linda, Dawn, and Wanda, Cindy, and Casey and Rollie. Those are the people that make this place work. On the other hand, it is my place to sell. I took the risks, I put in the hours. I laid out the money and I'm the one who has had enough. All the way home I keep thinking about the people who have been with me. Is it fair to them? I had an extra glass or two before I went to bed that night.

THE NEXT WEEK went by and I didn't see the offer on the table yet. Carl called and assured me that one was coming. I mentioned to Carl about the guilt pangs. He said that it happened to him every time he sold one of his businesses. For some reason it still didn't feel right, but I let it go until I had a firm offer in my hand.

After I finished up with Carl I got a call from my son. With all that was going on I almost forgot about our dinner. Fran told me that he and Nicole were good to go. We decided on Santapio's in East Boston. It's a dark, dingy hole in the wall directly under the exit ramp for the Callahan Tunnel. It is the home of the best pizza in Boston, as well as charbroiled lamb tips with hard bread and hot peppers. As good as the food is, the character of the restaurant is equally as intriguing. The stools have seen celebrities, mobsters, and even a murder or two. The efficient staff of waiters all have crooked noses and resemble a group of bookies from Suffolk Downs. They take your order on a three-by-five-inch unlined piece of white paper and I've never heard them ask anyone how much they've had to drink.

Even though a bar takes up half of the space of the restaurant, Santapio's serves a lot of families. Using foul language will get you a quick reminder from your friendly waiter, Rocco, that you could be floating with the fishes in Boston Harbor if you don't cut the crap. I've never seen our friend Rocco have to ask twice.

We decided to meet at the restaurant at six that evening. I stayed at work a little later to get myself organized for the following week. When I was walking out the door, Cindy picked up the phone. I gave her the "I already left" sign and she took a message. I stopped her in mid-lie when I heard it was Carl.

"Cindy is a hell of a secretary," Carl told me.

"Yeah, she also makes great whoopie."

"I have some news for you. Dimitri has made an offer and I think you might want to hear it."

"Fire away."

"He's offering $120,000 with $50,000 up front and finance $70,000 at 8 percent over five years. He said his offer will be on the table for seven days. I don't know if we could squeeze him for any more money, he seems pretty adamant about how he wants the deal structured. My guess is Uncle Spiro only wants to give him fifty grand. So what do you think?"

"I was hoping you'd get 75 up front. By the time I pay you and take care of any left over bills that would leave me about 50 grand to throw on the bed and roll naked in. I think I'm going to have to sleep on that offer, at least for the week. My first

95

inclination would be to make a counter offer. I'd let him have the purchase price of $120,000 but I'd need 60 up front and I'd finance the rest at 10% over five years."

"You know, Ian, I think he's making you a pretty good offer here. You might be better off tax-wise taking the 70 grand over the long period. You might want to give Vernon a call and ask him about that."

"You know, that's a good point, but Alan advised me to take at least half up front." Pausing for a minute I think, Jesus Christ, someone's actually going to be giving me money? I should be kissing his hairy ass and driving him to work everyday.

Carl interrupts my thoughts. "I told Dimitri I'd give him a call after I talked to you. What would you like me to tell him?"

"Thank him for the offer and tell him I'll need to talk to my accountant and lawyer about the tax ramifications of his proposal. As soon as I talk with them, I'll give him a yes, no, or a counter."

"So when do you think I'll hear from you?"

"By Monday at least but maybe sooner," I tell him.

Hanging up the phone, I gaze around the Honey Bee thinking about the big chunk of my life that I have worn into the concrete floors. Heading out the door, I wonder if I can look everybody in the eye if I decide to sell to Dimitri. Is it possible that I would miss the Honey Bee?

Opening the door to the Trooper, I hear the familiar whine of a banged-up Kia. As I look to the left there she is, Rotha. All the thoughts that have been running through my mind quickly flush away. All I can think is what a pleasure it would be to get rid of her ugly puss.

"Ian, we need to talk."

"You bet your fat ass we do." I barely notice her pathetic love interest, Leon, a security guard at the nuclear power plant, standing between myself and the high priestess of hideous.

"You know, I might have lost my cool the other day but I'm going to tell you something. That waitress of yours insulted me in front of all of my friends. All I did was ask her for a cup of coffee and she called me a bitch."

"Well, Rotha, she was wrong. You're not just a bitch, you're a big fucking ugly bitch and Casey couldn't have insulted you in front of all of your friends because you don't have any friends."

"You can't talk to me that way." I can see the steam rising from her head. I also see that Leon is staring at the ground just wanting the conversation to go away.

"I have a good mind to tell my husband what you're saying," Rotha continues.

"Go ahead and tell him. And while you're at it tell him that you're screwing Leon behind his back. I'd love to."

Leon starts to get real twitchy and finally opens his yap. "Can't you two just calm down," he says, trying to play the mediator.

I explain to Leon that I won't calm down and he and the wicked witch of the west ought to jump back on their broomstick and stay away from the Honey Bee for good.

Now Leon, dressed in his work uniform, security guard blue, decides to play cop. "You know, I've got a lot of friends on the force. You might want to reconsider your actions."

"Why thank you, Leon, I appreciate your thought. As a matter of fact, when I saw Rotha pull in my first inclination was to give her a good slap just like she gave Casey. But the sad fact is that I could never hit a woman, even one as ugly as her. However, I have come to the conclusion that I could use you as her surrogate." I realize that Leon is stumped by all of the long words so I give him a slap in the kisser.

Rotha starts howling about suing me for assault and Leon jumps right back in his car screaming that he's going to go down to the station and file charges.

It's only 3:30 and the perfect Honey Bee day has ended.

WHEN I ARRIVE home Emily greets me at the front door.

"The Seabrook police called and said you need to call them as soon as you get in. What the hell happened?"

I give her a quick play by play as I dial up the police station. I ask for Howard, a regular at the Bee.

"Hey Howard, this is Ian."

"Jesus, what the hell did you do? Leon was down here and wants to put you in the gas chamber."

"I know. That little homo just pissed me off."

"Well, the good news is that you didn't leave any marks and apparently Rotha was the only witness. But I am going to need you to come on down to the station."

"I'm just leaving to go to Boston to see my kids. Can I stop in tomorrow morning?"

"Okay, but we didn't have this conversation."

"Thanks Howard. I'll see you tomorrow. Any particular time?"

"Come in about nine. In the meantime I'll call Rotha and Leon and tell them that I put out an all points bulletin."

Setting down the phone I notice Emily ready to pounce.

"It seems you've had a busy day."

"You don't know how busy. I got an offer on the Honey Bee today."

"Already? How much was the offer for."

"One hundred and twenty thousand dollars. What do you think?"

"I thought you were asking for one fifty," she says in a disappointed tone.

"I know but that's the offer and it's on the table for seven days. I have to admit, I'm having second thoughts about selling to this guy, Dimitri. He wants to replace everybody with his Greek family. I just don't feel right about displacing all of the employees after all of these years."

"For Christ's sake, what are you thinking about? Think of all the fucking time and money and aggravation that you've poured into that place. This is a no brainer, it's time to think about what's good for us."

"That's exactly what I'm thinking about; what's best for us in the big picture."

"What's that supposed to mean?"

"Remember the last time we talked? Right as you were leaving for work you said that we were slipping away from each other and that you might be as guilty of it as me. Maybe you'd like to fill me in."

"Don't you have to get to Boston?" she asks.

"Yeah, I'm running late, we'll talk later."

SANTAPIO'S WAS just as dirty and delicious as ever. The kids were late as usual, so I enjoyed a couple of tall necks and a skewer of lamb. They finally arrived at 6:45 and we ordered a couple of pizzas and exchanged the usual phony pleasantries. Once the food arrived and we had a couple of drinks I cut to the chase.

"I just want you guys to know that there's going to be some changes. I think the Honey Bee is sold. If it is I'm going to take the summer off. I'll try to touch base with you from time to time. This is my way of making up for all of the vacations that I've missed in the last ten years."

Nicky asks, "Where are you going to go?"

"I don't know, it'll be my own personal road trip so I could end up anywhere."

"Is everything okay between you and Emily," my son inquires.

"I'm not sure, but she's just starting a new career and I'm due some time off. Look, you guys are at the age where you don't need me looking over your shoulder. If you need anything, I'll be in touch."

"Are you going to bring a cell phone with you?"

"No phone, no fax, no e-mail."

"This is all kind of sudden, isn't it?"

"No, it's been brewing for about forty eight years. If you ever have the luxury of working like a fucking mule and kissing as much ass as I have, you might want a summer off, too. Listen, I love you guys to death but you're acting like this is a funeral. This might be the best thing for me."

I know why they're nervous. The last time I left they were so young that they didn't know if they'd ever see me again. The sad part was that I didn't know if I'd ever see them again either. The only reason I came back was for them. I had to finish what I had created. My son is now twenty-five and taller than me. My daughter has two kids of her own. It's now time for them to reach for their own dreams and create their own messes.

Amid the paper plates and pizza crusts the tension starts to ease and we're back in our familiar roles. As we leave, I let them know that I'll contact them if anything transpires.

As I fight my way through Boston traffic heading north, I feel comforted to know that I can just let them go.

Heading over the Mystic River Bridge, I realize that the

Trooper had driven itself up Route 1 instead of Route 93, the quicker way home. This was a road that I had traveled many times through many failures and triumphs in my past life with my first wife.

The road is decorated with monuments to tacky. The giant orange dinosaur at the Saugus mini golf is down the road from the biggest Chinese restaurant in the East, Kowloon. Next is the huge neon cactus that is the home of the Hilltop Steak House. The fake Italian grass in the front is a corral for a life-size herd of cattle. Go a little further and Prince Spaghetti house is recognizable by the full-size replica of the Leaning Tower of Piza.

Each mile of Route 1 is a visual trip in a time machine. The building that used to house the Danish Massage is now an office building. I have fond memories of learning how to trade money for a blow job after my therapeutic massage. This was a valuable life lesson that never sank in. When I was about to get married the first time, my uncle Henry's advice was if you do the spending, they do the bending. Looking back I should have listened. For me, it was always love. What a fucking dope I was.

The glow from all of the gaudy signs and the memories have taken me away from an unbelievable day. Between the fight with Rotha and Leon, the offer, the kids, and Emily, the road and the neon are my therapy.

As the road merges with Route 95 there is one last beacon of salvation for weary men. The world famous Golden Banana is a gentleman's club. It's home of expensive drinks, silicone-enhanced strippers, and seedy patrons who look for a little titillation in their pathetic lives. I seem to fit right in with my brothers. It's been years since I stopped in, and things have changed. The stage is the same, the drinks still have more ice than liquor, and the bathroom should still be condemned. The real difference is in the strippers. I remember when they used to have some beautiful flaws. All of their boobs came in a variety of shapes and sizes. They used to actually perform an act to music before totally disrobing.

Today all of the strippers are eerily familiar. They're all a size 6. Their breasts resemble the Good Year blimp, all pumped-up by some medical marvel. Their acts now last about two minutes before they're totally naked. They all carry around that look that says "I'm too good for this place and I'm too good for you." The weirdest anomaly is that they are all clean-shaven of any ghastly pubic hairs. I yearn for the days when having a good bush was part of the mystique. Now they all remind me of a bunch of Chihuahuas.

Although my disdain is evident from what I've experienced this evening, I still pony up twenty dollars for a lap dance. My choice of dancers is Pearl who is in her early twenties with bottle-red hair and an ample chest. Beyond wearing just high heels and a g-string, there was nothing very extraordinary about her. Her performance was equally as unenthusiastic.

As uninspiring as she was, she was well worth the twenty dollars. In the middle of one of her poses, when I was trying to figure out if she could possibly be a natural redhead, an interesting idea hit me. If I had to sell the Honey Bee and I didn't want to see my staff decimated by Dimitri's clan, why shouldn't I sell it in-house? Guy would be the perfect foil for my plan. In a lot of ways we are very similar. He learned about women the hard way from a disastrous first marriage. We are similar in stature. He's still young enough to take the punishment from the Honey Bee. He genuinely likes people, unlike myself. The staff respects him, the customers like him, and his most important aspect is that he shows up. The rest he can figure out as he goes along. On the downside, he probably doesn't have the cash to get into the business. This would not please Emily and Carl but I could look past it.

As Pearl finishes up, I feel obligated to tip her a twenty spot. She thanked me but was surprised. She said that I didn't look like I was enjoying myself very much. I told her I wasn't but that I came up with a great fucking idea and learned a valuable lesson. A man always does his best thinking when he's on a beaver hunt. I knew she was confused by my epiphany so I left before any more painful conversation could take place.

It was 12:30 and I headed straight for the Honey Bee to talk with Guy, who was currently making donuts. He was surprised by my knock on the back door.

"Ian, what's wrong?"

"This is going to sound funny but I was getting a lap dance down at the Banana and I thought of you."

"I appreciate the thought but I am strictly hetero."

"Don't worry, you're not my type either. The reason I was thinking of you was that I received an offer on the Honey Bee. It's a Greek family and they want to come in and take everybody's place. I'm really struggling with this offer because as much as I piss and moan about this place, I like it and the people that work here. I'm going to have to make the decision to sell or not by the end of the week."

Guy looks dumbfounded and says, "I didn't even know you were selling."

"I had to keep it quiet, you know how news travels around here. Anyways, while I was sitting there having a beer and enjoying some tang I came up with an excellent idea. Rather than sell this place to some hairy-back Greek, I'll take a shot at selling it to you."

He takes a moment to absorb what I have said. He begins to wonder out loud if he could do it or not. I quickly assure him that ninety percent of what I do is just hard work. The rest would be easy to learn because I would teach him. He immediately jumps to his next concern.

"How much money would you be looking for?"

"I'd be looking for the whole fucking sum but I know that's not going to happen. I'll need some dough but if you're interested, I'll keep it reasonable."

"How much is reasonable?"

"Well, I was trying to sell it for $150,000. Carl was selling it for me. He found this guy, Dimitri, and he made an offer for $120,000, 50 down and 70 financed. I know you would have a hard time coming up with that money but I would need some."

I can see him start to drift when I mention numbers, like it's all a bit overwhelming.

I say, "You know, Guy, you'd make a pretty good living out of this place. It has paid for my house, the kid's college, and lots of toys and trinkets. I think someone single like yourself with no kids could do very well. Look at it this way, for the price of that brand new truck you bought, you could own the Honey Bee. I'll make sure the payments are reasonable. I'll even work for you for a month to get you headed in the right direction."

"Jesus, this is all so sudden, you caught me off guard."

"Don't worry, I don't need an answer today. Sleep on it and we'll talk in a couple days."

"There is something I would like to ask you. What are you planning on doing after you sell?"

"I'm taking the summer off. I'm going to start at Bike Week in Laconia and raise nothing but pure hell until Labor day."

"How does Emily feel about that?"

"I don't know. You want to give her a call and find out?"

"So I take it things are going well at home."

"Today they are because I am not there."

"I'm sorry to hear that."

"I'll talk to you in a couple days. If you have any questions give me a call. If not, I'll see you Friday morning."

THE NEXT morning I had to be down at the police station bright and early. Although my brain was running on empty I had already figured out how to get my ass out of that sling.

I saw Howard at the station and told him that if Leon was nice enough to drop the charges against me then I would not have Casey press charges against that baboon-faced bitch, Rotha. Howard gave Leon a call at the Nuke plant and the deal was made.

After the police station, I swing by Carl's house to give him a head's up about the proposed deal with Guy. With all that's going on it feels great to be on the bike again.

Carl greets me at his front door with, "This is a surprise. What the hell are you doing here?"

"I was wondering if we could talk for a few minutes but first I'd like to show you something."

Carl and I head down his front steps and I proudly show him my black beauty. "Wow, that's nice. How does it feel to have your dream bike?"

"You don't know how good. I remember you used to always tell me that somebody who works hard should be able to treat himself well. I guess I started to finally do it. The real reason I came down was to talk about Dimitri's offer. In one way I'm really tempted to accept it but greed isn't the only factor. There are a lot of people that work for me that I consider friends and if Dimitri buys the place, they all would be dismissed. I'm not feeling real good about that scenario."

"Ian, I think you're making a mistake. No job is for an eternity. Besides, you should treat yourself to the best offer."

"That's why I'm here. I think what would be best for me and the Honey Bee is if I keep the sale in-house."

Carl looks puzzled and says, "Well, what are you thinking?"

"I'd like to have Guy buy it."

"Where's he going to get the dough?"

"That's the only problem. I'd have to find a way to work with him on that and I was hoping you'd help me so I could get it done."

"What are you proposing?"

"You find a way to work with Guy, I'll give you $2,000 up front and the other three grand I'll split into three payments."

"Are you sure this is what you want to do?"

"I couldn't be more positive. It came to me as a vision while I was having a lap dance at the Golden Banana."

Carl smiles. "Listen, I'll help you any way I can but let's ride out the week to see if Guy is up to it. At least you'll have Dimitri as a fall back."

"Okay, I'll be talking to Guy on Friday and then I'll give you a call."

FRIDAY I PULL in at the Bee at 5 A.M. I am a little nervous about seeing Guy, just hoping that his decision was positive. We give each other our usual greeting.

"Guy, I only have one question for you. Can I leave now?"

Guy smiles and says, "Not right this minute, but I'm working on it."

Guy's response meant that for the first time in ten years I could work at the Honey Bee for a whole day with a shit-eating grin on my face. It felt so good to know that the people that make the Bee special would remain.

Although it took a month to consummate the deal, I saw Guy grow into his new position and I felt confident that I had made the right decision.

During that month I also took my leave of absence from the newspaper. Although I will miss writing and the battles with my editor, the clock was ticking on my personal cleansing.

Things were not going so well at home. Emily didn't like my decision to sell the Honey Bee to the lowest bidder. She was spending more and more time at work. I could feel the influence of the Professor slowly invading her. I left her a note telling her the sale would be completed the Friday after Memorial Day. I invited her to come. She didn't answer my note.

With time running short, I stayed home late one morning to catch Emily before she left. She was surprised to see me sitting at the kitchen table with a coffee in my hand.

"I didn't hear from you, I wondered if you wanted to go to the closing with me on Friday."

"Why would I want to do that? I didn't participate in any of your other decisions."

"Yeah, I know I kept you out of the loop on this."

"It's not just this, you keep me out of everything."

"I thought participation went two ways. I get the feeling that you only wanted to participate on your own terms."

"Living with you, it might be called self-preservation."

"You're right, but the truth is that we're both fading away from each other. There's no one to blame. It's life pulling us in different directions."

"Do you really believe that or is it an excuse for your middle-age madness?" she asks.

"Before we start speaking in tongues, can we focus on what's the truth? The truth is I am unhappy with my life. We are slowly slipping into becoming the couple that is more convenient than passionate. The truth is that I don't want to get old. I hate my work and I feel incomplete. The truth is I'll always love you but I can never give you the attention you need. I know the Professor has replaced me in your dreams and I won't fight it."

"What the hell are you talking about?"

"I read your journal. I found it the day I went to that card game a couple of months ago. I didn't confront you because it wouldn't have changed anything. These are the things I know. Right now, I need my summer. You need yours. Maybe this is a good thing for us. I don't know, but I'm willing to take the risk to find out."

Emily asks, "Why did it take so long for the truth?"

"Fear. The truth is the one thing that we're all scared of."

The conversation I dreaded was now over. Emily left for work. On this bleakest of days I went to my barn and watched a cold rain fall. I pulled the ragged memo card from my wallet. My checklist was now complete. All I had to do was tie up a few loose ends. Bike Week was almost here.

My new life would start with a clean slate. I would have one more chance of resurrecting lost dreams. At least this time I'm leaving the truth behind instead of fear, pain, and lies. These were my Armageddon days.

Chapter 3: Resurrection

I'M NOW ON THE CUSP of leaving for my new life. Before I get on that road, I must clean up and organize the last remnants of my old life. While all of the main components are in place, it's the fucking details that always drive me crazy.

Emily left this morning for her seminar in Nova Scotia with Professor Romeo. Our last conversations were muted by our desire to get on with our lives. My curiosity brought me to the brink of reopening her journal. I stopped myself when I realized it would be cheating. She let me go for the summer without any rules or requirements. As usual I was looking to be one up. I always took pride in being a step ahead of anyone I was involved with, at any cost. As much as leaving is about grabbing for a dream, it's even more about an evolution of character. This is a final chance to remake those old flaws.

In two days I will be leaving. As I look at the collection of items I have accumulated, it is overwhelming. It is so easy to talk about simplifying until you're actually faced with it. Thousands of trinkets that I could never live without would be tomorrow's trash. All that was important now had to fit in one milk crate. That is all the bike would allow for storage. This simplest of tasks would turn out to be the hardest over the next days.

I need to get a sleeping bag and a Swiss Army knife so I

head over to a local Army-Navy store to buy what would now be my home for the summer.

I tell Dave, the owner of the store, I am looking for a heavy-duty bag because I will be camping outside for most of the summer. He informs me that I will need more than a bag to be comfortable. He recommends an air mattress, tent, Coleman lamp, canteen, and assorted Boy Scout paraphernalia. I tell him that I can take none of that because I will be on a motorcycle. Dave looks at me curiously and says, "I bet you're about my age. If you don't mind me asking, why would you want to be sleeping outside the whole summer? I do a lot of camping and you're setting yourself up for one cold, wet summer."

"Well, Dave, that's why I'm here. People told me you're the expert. My motorcycle is right outside and you can take a look at the luggage rack on the back. That will be the space allowed for the Hanoi Hilton you can fix me up with."

Dave looks over the bike and shrugs his shoulders. "You're asking the impossible."

"Well do what's possible."

He shakes his head and goes back into the store. He spends half an hour dragging stuff out to the motorcycle and seeing what he can squeeze in. After a lot of head shaking, Dave has everything lined up on his counter. He explains that what he has performed is a miracle. He has picked an ultra-light waterproof tent that resembles a cocoon. His choice of sleeping bag looks military standard. He explains that it is army state-of-the-art. There is a thin nippled piece of padding that is textured like an egg crate. He also includes a nylon zippered waterproof case. He explains that this is the best part and I would thank him someday. The camouflaged case contains a flashlight, waterproof matches, razor wire for cutting down small trees for kindling, a first aid kit, and a Swiss Army knife. He takes everything and rolls it into a black waterproof pouch. He proudly walks out to the motorcycle with it. He has two nylon straps with plastic buckles attached. He places the pouch on top of the chrome luggage rack and uses the two straps like bungee cords to secure the pouch. He says that the straps will come in handy for everything from keeping groceries out of reach of animals to hanging clothes to dry to carrying wood.

Dave is a little pricey but well worth it. When I leave I head back to my house to try to complete my packing. I start by putting my wallet on the kitchen table. What once was a thin billfold is now loaded with credit cards, various ID's, rolling papers, business cards, and a thin string of beads borrowed from Masconomet's grave. The business cards are first to hit the trash, each and every one of them would be useless to me now. Next I call the numbers on the backs of the credit cards to cancel them. I keep my license, my credit card-sized diploma from Gloucester High, and my rolling papers. The beads I string around the base of my handlebars, next to the tachometer.

As I put only the necessities back in my wallet I remember that it's also going to carry my cash for the summer. It will be just as fat and awkward as it was before I relieved it of all its trash. I have never lost my wallet before probably because I never left cash in it. Since I would be traveling, I would be screwed if I lost my license and cash. I decide to go visit my friend, Art, and invest in one of those wallets that I always said I'd never wear. It's a big black billfold with a chain attached, the ones that are usually worn by wannabe bad boys and greasers.

I haven't seen Art in a while so I bring him up to date on all the changes that have taken place for me. He isn't surprised but a little pissed that I haven't let him know sooner. He is also sad about the passing of my newspaper article, of which he was a vocal critic.

"So what the fuck am I going to read now, Dear Abby?" Art exclaims.

"Just drag out your old copies of *Gay Biker Magazine* and head to the bathroom. Are you going to be up at Laconia?"

"Yeah, I'm going to be selling there over the weekend down at the tents by the drive-in. Check in with me, we'll go out some night."

"That sounds great but today I need your expertise. I'm going to be away all summer and I need one of those wallets with the chains on them, you know, the kind that all the fucking idiots wear."

"You mean the kind I wear, shithead?"

"Yeah, that's the kind. Let me ask you a question, Art. Are those things really necessary? Is there any way I could hide the chain so I don't look like one of those freaks?"

"Let me explain something to you, Mr. Middle-age Crazy. If you want to look good, go out and buy a hairpiece. If you don't want to lose your wallet then step over here and buy one of these fine Art's Cow Parts creations. Besides, the really sleazy biker chicks just love chain wallets, it makes them horny."

"So are you guaranteeing that I get laid if I buy this wallet?"

"No, not as ugly as you are, but I am guaranteeing you won't lose your wallet."

Art and I spend another half-hour shooting the shit and insulting one another. When I leave I have a new wallet. The chain dangles from my side but I don't even notice it is there until I jump on the bike. I realize that I am now one of those losers with one of those wallets.

I head back to my house to attempt to fill up the milk crate that gives me the same amount of space as my saddlebags. I know why I kept avoiding this project. Even though it is just for the summer, I feel sad that I can put all of my worldly possessions in a small, plastic crate. I start with six pairs of socks and underwear, my five favorite T-shirts, three pairs of jeans, two turtlenecks, rain gear, a toothbrush and toothpaste, and soap. I push everything down so I can try to squeeze in a few more articles but I decide against it to leave space for the chaps and leather jacket which will have to be stored in extreme heat.

While the milk crate seems to be full, it is empty of mementoes. I've always kept little pieces of my past to drag out for personal medication and amusement. I've never been a "picture in the wallet" guy so I grab the velvet pouch that a bottle of Crown Royal comes in and scour the house for some strange remembrances.

The first item is a small postcard advertisement for one of my son's shows called "Dream Dancing." Fran and his friend, Paul, do this act once a year at a club in Boston. It's about as high-end art, theatre, and music that you can get in one show and each year my son pours his heart into it.

Next I cut a section of my daughter's old blanket that she never let go of for the first eight years of her life. Looking back at that period of time, I used to think that things would be normal, that I could have a nuclear family and fit into the social norm. Today it seems like believing in Santa Claus or the Easter Bunny. Her blanket was like a bad omen, the minute she left it behind the family fell apart.

Last and most important I have to take something of Emily's. She was the best and I owe her. I love her. I let her down. There is so much that I could take, love letters, notes, jewelry, but none of these would do. Rummaging around I find an old T-shirt from Salisbury Beach. It is black with fringes, too tight and low-cut. It was exactly the opposite of Emily. I remember when we bought it. We were at the beach daydreaming about our future. The hot sun and cold beer led us to Salisbury and a shopping spree at the Salisbury Discount House, from cheap jewelry to tacky T-shirts and flip flops to chic bathing suits. Walking out with a bag of goodies each, we changed into our new outfits in the little booth where you take Polaroid's. We now looked like Salisbury regulars. We ate pizza at Tripoli's, did shots at the Normandy, and played Skeeball at Joe's Playland. I could have stayed there forever that day. Emily was always elegant, but that day she was exotic. The world of her self-fulfillment seemed far away. The shirt comes with me along with the memory.

Now all that I have to do is finishing touches on my packing. I have almost forgotten to bring a little marijuana in case of a medical emergency. I also needed a fresh deck of 'Boro's, a package of playing cards, a pocket-sized .22 caliber derringer, and a flask of Crown Royal. I can now be stranded anywhere for any number of days and be content. I take a test run bringing everything out to the motorcycle. To my amazement, everything fits into the two saddlebags with room to spare.

THE NEXT MORNING I need to go visit Guy to clean up the last details of our deal. I pull into the Honey Bee and I realize that I am now an intruder. The parking lot is still full of cars. People are still hanging around out front and conversing in their Seabrook dialect.

Is it possible that I was actually a replaceable part? I always felt like I was the only one who could ever do my job and if I left for more than two days the Honey Bee would sink into oblivion. Apparently this was not the case because when I slip in the back door everything is rolling along like I had never left. Guy has grown a little older over the past month trying to take on so much in such a short time frame. It is now the Honey

Bee's turn to toughen up Guy. If history repeats itself, he will be there for more than a handful of years, in which time his hair will get gray, his legs will get tired, and he'll become a cynical bastard.

Guy is standing at the stainless steel bench looking over a pile of paperwork.

"Hey bossman, how are things?" I greet.

Guy looks exasperated. "The ladies' room is overflowing, the Coke refrigerator's on the blink, and Casey called in sick."

"Well, I'm glad to hear things are going good. Would you like a hand? I'm not leaving until tomorrow."

"No, that's okay. I don't want to bother you."

"It's no bother, let's get to it. We'll do the bathroom first, it sounds like the easiest to fix. You go to the men's room, I'll go to the ladies room, and we'll double plunge."

"Why am I going in the men's room? It's the ladies room that's fucked up," Guy says.

"It always gets blocked up where the two pipes meet and if you plunge the crap out of both of them at the same time, like a miracle all of your troubles will be flushed away."

After about ten minutes of slopping away, we now hear the beautiful gurgling sound that says, "Ladies and Gentlemen, you are now free to flush." I could see a little relief starting to creep into Guy's negative mindset as we approached the broken refrigerator.

"This thing's just not cold enough," Guy explains.

After twenty-five years of owning restaurants, I've been screwed over by every refrigeration guy that ever walked through the door. After the first couple of times of being ripped off, I started to watch what they did. After a short period of time, I started to pick up some of their tricks. I eventually did a lot of my own repairs.

"Okay, Guy, the first trick to working on any piece of re-frigeration is to take off your belt. That way when you're bend-ing down to work, everyone can see the crack of your ass. That is the only common denominator that I have found among all those refrigeration pirates. This particular fridge is tempera-mental. When it gets tired or runs out of gas, the condenser freezes up and the temperature rises." I direct Guy's hand to the block of ice that's formed on the unit. "If you let it thaw until the ice melts then when you turn it back on it should run fine. After that, adjust the temperature down a hair. If it freezes up again, call the guy with the hairy ass to put some gas in it."

I know Guy's a little skeptical because it was always a joke at the Honey Bee that I wasn't mechanically inclined.

"Any ideas on filling in Casey's shift today?" Guy asks.

"Sure, just ask yourself this question: since I've left, who's been buttering you up? You know, kissing your ass for no good reason."

"What do you mean?" Guy was never quick on the draw.

"There's always someone who is extra nice to the boss. Who has that been?"

"It's Dawn, I guess."

"Yeah, she's always been kind of sweet on you, hasn't she? But let me ask you this: what about the floater? You know, the lazy eye?"

"Actually," Guy answers, "this might sound funny, but I kind of like it."

"No shit? Damn, that's cool. Surprise, surprise. The Guy man's a bit kinky. Have you been boning her or what?"

"No, it's nothing like that," Guy assures me.

"Okay, then your problem is solved. Just give Dawn a call and put on that pathetic 'I'm a lost little puppy dog' voice of yours and say, 'jeez, I know it's last minute and you probably can't do it but Casey's out today and I was wondering if you could help.'"

Three minutes later, Guy puts down the phone and the last of his problems is solved. Now that the pressure is off and I have his attention, we begin to take care of the last details of our agreement.

"I set up an account at the bank across the street," I tell Guy. "That way you just put the mortgage payment in there every month. You're going into your busy season so you really shouldn't have any problem paying. If by any chance you do have a problem, just leave a message at my house. I'll be touching base there every once in a while. Other than that, I cashed your check for the $20,000. I know how much money that is for someone like yourself. I also know there'll be days like this one when you'll say, "why the fuck did I buy this place?' but I think you'll find over the long term that the Bee will treat you pretty good."

"Thanks, I appreciate your help," Guy says.

"There's only one last thing I need to do. Come here, I want to show you something. Today I'm taking my secret stash. At the end of every day I've owned the Honey Bee I took ten dollars and put it in a little strong box behind this panel that pops out. Carl did the same before me. See, if all else fails, if your dog runs off, your wife's screwing the mailman, the IRS is going to audit you, you will still have your stash. The wife doesn't know about it and best of all, your silent partner Uncle Sam doesn't know about it."

I pull out the strong box and it is stuffed with ten-dollar bills.

Guy says, "That's a lot of goddamned money."

"Not really. What it is is a lot of goddamned long days."

Guy helps me count out all of the money and it totals $12,130.

"So what are you going to spend all of your money on?" Guy inquires.

"I have to give Carl two grand, that was our agreement when we didn't sell it to the Greeks. I'm giving Emily two grand for the summer. The rest I'm going to donate to my favorite charity. Me."

Guy chuckles and says, "How generous."

We head out the back door sharing a few more laughs. I tell him that I'll see him at the end of the summer. Guy thanks me for the opportunity that I made possible for him. We shake hands and I pull out of the Honey Bee thinking it should have been the other way around. I should be the one thanking him. I get to enjoy a summer off while he gets to work his ass off.

I stop at the bank to cash in all of the ten dollar bills for traveler's checks and big bills. I hate banks and I hate tellers. The most loathsome of these creatures is the head teller, Penny. She's overly helpful, overly nice, and overly phony. I dread going up to her window. First, she butchers my name and then as I'm leaving, she insists on telling me, "You have the best day you've ever had!" I never respond to this bitch. I always walk out with one thought, the best day I could ever have is if someone robbed this bank, and after Penny rounded up all of the money and wished them a super day, they would shoot her in some senseless act of mercy so no one would have to listen to her heartfelt greetings.

I swing by Carl's after. He is busy sprucing up his camper for the upcoming Nascar season. He gleefully counts his twenty hundred-dollar bills twice. He admits that I probably did the right thing by selling to Guy. As much as Carl can look at something in a cold, calculated, business-like way, he is actually a marshmallow.

Carl lets me know that his dream of moving to Florida is

finally a reality. It is sad to think that this might be the last time that I see him. Owning the Honey Bee is a little like going to war. Not only were Carl and I friends and partners, but we thrived on and survived all of the battles of the Bee.

I HEAD UP TO Portsmouth to start my tattooing. I've decided to start with my shoulders. The left shoulder will symbolize my birth with the Egyptian symbol for life. The other shoulder will don a design of a sarcophagus, an elaborate Egyptian coffin, with a birdman hovering over it. This symbolizes the freeing of the human soul and death.

Five hundred dollars and four hours later the bookends of my life story were complete. Jason, my tattoo artist, inquires if I will be continuing my tale with more tattoos on my torso. I tell him that I will be back and that I am still filling in some of the story. I explain to Jason that some of it hasn't happened yet.

As I jump on the bike, I don't know what direction to go in. I am leaving in the morning and a good night's sleep wouldn't hurt. I just don't want to go home to an empty house and question myself all night. The sun is just going down and my mood is following it. I drag my sorry disposition into the Muddy River, a Portsmouth smokehouse with forty beers on tap. Although I love the River, most of the beers suck, particularly the brown ones that pour like pancake syrup and don't taste much better. Luckily they carry a few brands of normal beer.

Pabst Blue Ribbon is my choice for the evening that will last too long. I am now single in my thought process and I make a point to flirt with every pair of tits in the place. I have been out of circulation so long that I need to practice.

This night I am an utter failure but that's good. It's a numbers game. If you hit on twenty women there will at least be two who will give you a try as long as you're not Frankenstein-ugly, foul-smelling, or talk like you have a mouth full of nuts. Four women didn't get lucky at the River. So next time my odds increase to score. The hardest part is the ego. There are so many men that just can't handle the rejection. One try and they wrap it up for the night. Others will try more than once but after one "no" the pressure's on. That guy will get out of skin to get some ass. He will lie about everything from what he does and how much he makes to how big his little chubby is. It's like a baseball player with two strikes in the ninth inning, he's swinging at everything. This inevitably ends in disaster.

I make it a point to only engage women who smile and at least look interesting. Beauty is highly overrated. Give me some geeky broad with a smile that's not a passenger of the Xanax train anytime over a frown-faced Barbie doll. I want busty, lusty, and musty anytime over perfumed and prissy. I did realize one new important fact: my looks have changed over time and the women that might give me a try will look different from the ones in my past.

The ride home that night is a bitch. I forget how much drinking diminishes your skills on a motorcycle. Lots of beers give you lots of balls. Most motorcycle accidents are caused by two reasons: alcohol and some fucking idiot in a car that doesn't look. If you don't respect both of these dangers then one of them will eventually get you.

I take back roads at the speed limit but that doesn't stop me from my first scare on the new bike. Going about 40 mph, a truck hits its brakes to avoid a dog. I feel like I am a safe distance behind the four-by-four but the light rain this evening makes the road a touch slick. I lock up my breaks and start to skid. In slow motion I watch the back of the truck creep toward me. Then I remember that Harley Davidson gave me five gears. Downshifting and turning I stop alongside the truck with a wet spot on my jeans. At home that night I keep reliving the controlled slide my new bike gave me. A smaller machine would have laid down but my new beast had balls. I also have to promise to remind myself of the thinking and not drinking oath that bikers take after a near miss.

It is a restless night. The good memories of Emily invade me at every toss and turn. I am relieved when the sky starts to lighten. Anxious to hit the road, with rain in the forecast and temperatures in the low fifties, I double-check my baggage and throw in my toothbrush, a comb, razor, and soap. I dress for a long, cold ride to Laconia. This will be my first full Bike Week. I have been up as a day spectator but now is my turn to raise hell with the other bikers. I give myself one quick look before I head out. The tattoos, leathers, and long goatee give me pause at the total metamorphosis that has taken place in the past few months.

I leave Emily a short note letting her know that the money from the Bee will be deposited by Guy on the first of each month and that I left two bills in our cash spot for her summer. There is no need to get weird or regretful so I just keep it to the point and tell her I love her and I will be thinking of her.

My last act is to take a piss in the water bowl in Caesar's dog house. He is spending the week in a kennel while Emily is away. I feel this little gift will let Caesar know how much I'll miss him.

I PULL OUT OF the driveway and don't look back. I can already hear the roar of motorcycles heading north on Route 125. They will not be leaving me behind this time. At the stoplight they just keep coming, all shapes and sizes. The drizzle is starting so everyone is at warp speed before the heavy rain. My destination is Naswa beach resort, a motel and cottage complex right on Lake Winnipesaukee, about a quarter mile from Weirs Beach where all the activity would be. I have stayed there once before and their Tiki bar on the beach is a great place to get a noon buzz. The price is a screw job but I had gotten the room the day after I bought the bike. I didn't know then that I would be off for the whole summer so I was willing to pay anything at the time.

The line of motorcycles grows with each and every mile that passes. There are digital construction signs cautioning motorists to watch for motorcycles. The police details are mostly on bikes looking for morning buzzers and speeders. For the most part the ride is slow and the bikes are two abreast as far as I can see by the time I hit Alton Bay at the tip of the lake. With fifteen miles still to go, the Harleys now rule the road. Fatboys, hogs, speedsters, and Road Kings are all tweaked by their equally diverse owners. There are fat guys, skinny guys, short ones and tall ones. Some are blond, some are bald. Some are shaven and others have long beards. They are from every state in the northeast and some drove even further. The one common denominator in this melting pot of hell on wheels is attitude. The mindset is half-patriot, half-pirate. The Jolly Roger should be their national flag. Laconia will be their capital for the next week and all the police are really referees and EMTs. The land of SUV's and minivans is now ruled by EVO's and miniskirts.

As we get closer to Weirs Beach, signs on every campground and motel read, "Bikers Welcome." This is exactly the opposite of what you would find in most resort areas. Most innkeepers have an unwritten rule: if you're on two wheels, no vacancy. This misperception is harbored by the fear of the uptight middle-class. Their stereotype of a biker is of a drug dealing, tattooed wild-man who would steal their daughter, their cash, and their way of life. Nothing could be farther from the truth. Motorcycle enthusiasts are diverse, they could be bankers, waitresses, or software engineers. This is their outlet. It's more of a lifestyle than a hobby. You'll know if you're addicted the first time you get on a bike. The road, the danger, and the freedom will either intoxicate you or terrify you.

When I hit the top of the hill overlooking Weirs, the roar is deafening. The flashing neon Weirs Beach sign is where all of the traffic converges from every direction. As you approach this intersection you expect mayhem. Instead there are simple nods that take the place of traffic lights. The traffic cop is as good as a dummy in the road. The true order comes from the respect that one biker gives to another. As much traffic as there seems to be, this is only the first day. The rain has kept the crowd extremely light. Even though every part of my body is drenched and shivering, I join the rest of the masses in a quick trip up the half-mile strip that serves as the parade route for the thousands of motorcycles.

Weirs Beach is a small honky-tonk resort on the south side of Lake Winnipesaukee. It has a sandy beach that is bordered by railroad tracks. On the opposite side of the street, there is a collection of candy-colored Victorian hotels that overlook the great lake. Toward the end of the strip, the scenery changes. The funky nineteenth century homes end and a string of arcades, gift shops, and saloons begins. Across the street from these is a boardwalk and dock. This is where the *Mt. Washington* picks up tourists for scenic summertime cruises. The ticket office also doubles as a railroad station.

During Bike Week, Weirs is totally transformed into a tent city. Shopping has taken precedence over the motorcycle races, which years ago were the main attraction. The races have found a new home at the New Hampshire International Speedway. The Speedway was built for Nascar events. Holding the mo-

torcycle races at this giant venue has diminished their uniqueness.

In less than three minutes, my ride down the Hollywood
Boulevard of Bike Week is over. I can't wait to get around the
corner to the hotel and peel off my wet clothes. When I check
in all I can do was shiver as I fill out all of the idiotic paperwork
to secure my home for the week. My thoughts of running down
to the Tiki bar are replaced by a long, hot shower. Even though
the trip to Laconia only took two hours, I feel like I have been
riding for a week. The warm water and quiet room leave me
counting sheep, resting up for the week of festivities ahead.

Four hours later I awake to the sound of driving rain outside my window. Rather than be left with my own insecurities,
I decide to make my way down to the small bar inside the hotel.
There are already about a dozen early arrivals at the bar. The
uniforms of the patrons are T-shirts from past Laconia Bike
Weeks. It is their way of letting you know that they are not
rookies. As outgoing and curious as I usually am, tonight I will
use my barstool as an observation post, waiting for somebody
to approach me rather than initiating.

As the beer flows freely, I don't have to wait long. The
groups that are separated by unfamiliarity change to a chorus
of Where are you from? What are you driving? What are you
drinking? Even a skeptical prick like myself finds it easy to
bounce from group to group. Not one person asks, "What do
you do?" This is contrary to normal social procedure. It was so
different to find people who were curious about who you are
rather than what you do.

As evening wears on, I become tired of going from stool
to stool and table to table. I anchor myself to a table of bikers
from Vermont. There is Will and his wife, Jeannie. Will is in
his mid-forties, about six feet tall with a shaved head. He wears

a black leather vest adorned with souvenir pins from his travels from Quebec to Daytona. The vest is draped around an ample gut that gives him a Buddha look. He has an easy smile that says, "I'm just happy to be out of fucking Vermont."

His wife Jeannie is bottle-blond with a plump but well-defined frame. She wears a lot of turquoise and a fringed leather jacket. To the casual observer her biggest and best asset is her full rack. It keeps falling on the table whenever she reaches for the pitcher of beer. When this occurs, Will's grin becomes even more content like he is making an offering to the tit-God.

The third wheel in this group is Jeannie's friend, Samantha. She is the introvert in this Green Mountain triad. Her long, dirty-blond hair is pulled back in a single braid that hangs all the way to her ass. She is only about 5 foot 3, but her body is strong and muscular. She is probably on the downside of thirties, with small hands and a soft face. Her smile isn't as easy as her friends. I like how Samantha is dressed. There is nothing to read on her black T-shirt and her leather jacket is for riding rather than something out of Cher's closet. We are the only two that night who have not dressed for the occasion. I wonder if this is an oversight or a sign.

As the evening goes on, the table becomes filled with pitchers. The conversation is easier with each fill up. While Will, Jeannie, and myself are easy to expose, Sam keeps in the shadows, listening but not joining in.

I can't remember the last time I made it to last call. My inner clock is finally adjusting to life without the Honey Bee. As Will and I are killing off the last pitcher, he invites me to join them for a ride around the lake the next day.

I crawl up to my room to a sloshing sound that resembles a half-empty keg being tossed about. As bloated as I am, I go to sleep easily, content that I have made friends on the first day of my new life.

I MEET WILL, Jeannie, and Sam in the lobby around eleven. We all seem to be carrying the aftereffects of the night before and are in no big rush to get going. The rain has finally stopped although it is still foggy. The sun seems to be trying to push through. We grab some coffees and go outside to dry our motorcycles. Will and Jeannie drive a full dresser which seems to be a perfect match for their size. Sam has a sportster. There is nothing really unique about it but it is tight, strong, and easy to respect. I have not ridden with a lot of female bikers—this seems to be a recent phenomenon. Years ago, female riders were presumed to be dikes. This is no longer the case.

Will and Jeannie lead the way as we left the parking lot. Sam and I tail behind, side by side. She doesn't fade from one side to the other, her turns are tight and confident. Her riding is aggressive yet controlled. I never would have got this from the night before. Maybe she is just a show-me gal and what she is showing me is a peek at her personality.

The sun finally starts to break through the clouds as we roll through Meredith. This quaint New England village is the total opposite of Weirs. Subarus topped with kayaks rule the roads that are lined with candle stores and antique shops. As we cruise through the town, we can see the homies thinking, "Oh Jesus, it's Bike Week again." I've always loved that look from people I drive by. It makes you want to have the loudest bike the law will allow just to piss them off.

We continue our journey around the northern outskirts of the lake, hitting all of the "boros," Moultenborough, Peterborough, and Wolfeboro. Will and Jeannie bring us up to a beautiful outlook in Peterborough called Castle in the Clouds. The road weaves its way up a mountain to a replica of an English castle built into the mountaintop. The view overlooks all of Winnipesaukee and, on clear days, you can see Boston.

We make our way back to Alton Bay, almost completing our circle. We once again join the long line of bikes heading into Laconia. When we get back to town we decide to stop in an Irish pub on the other side of the airport, about four miles from where we're staying. O'Leary's is your standard Irish saloon stuck in a strip mall. The décor is typically early leprechaun. The beer of the day is a black and tan. We don't bite on our Irish surroundings; we order a couple of pitchers of Bud and four shots of Tequila to toast our trip. As we raise our Tequilas to toast, Will says, "Here's to a good week and meeting a new friend."

Jeannie leans over and gives me a squeeze. "You're not as big a dink as everyone says you are." We all start laughing but I am thinking, I couldn't be too big of a dink yet, I haven't had the chance.

Will says, "Wasn't it a great ride around the lake?"

To everyone's surprise we hear a new voice join the conversation when Sam says, "I would have enjoyed the ride a lot more if I didn't have a male driver next to me. You know how they are."

Feeling playful, I say, "Damn, it speaks! I thought you were a mute."

Sam responds, "Well maybe I only speak when I have something to say."

Will and Jeannie start howling at our short exchange. Will chimes in, "Listen, Ian, this is the most she's spoken since we left. I'm hoping some of the silence rubs off on Jeannie."

"For Christ's sake, nobody has a bigger mouth than you, Will," Jeannie says.

"You love it," he says as he gives her a big lick on the side of her face. The pitchers are now empty. Jeannie and Sam go off to the ladies room as Will and I order another round. I now seize the opportunity to inquire about Sam.

"Will, what's with Sam? How come she's up here alone?"

"She's a little tough to get to know but she's worth it. Look at it this way, if you hook up with Sam, I get to get laid because we're all sharing a room."

"What's the matter, no double-headers?"

"No such luck," Will says.

As the girls walk back to the table, Will and I are grinning like Cheshire cats.

Jeannie says, "What the fuck are you guys grinning at? Haven't you ever seen good-looking broads before?"

We suck up our next round as quickly as our first. We head back to the hotel. Before I retire to my room, I promise them that I'd touch base with them the next day to see what was going on.

WHEN I GET back to my room, I give Leo, my long lost friend, a call. We used to chum around as kids and he now lives with his family in Sweden, Maine. I make plans to go visit him the next day.

I figure I'll head down to the beer tents to see if there is any action at the clubs. Things are just starting to gear up by Saturday night, a lot of the bigger motorcycle clubs have shown up and they are eager to raise hell.

I bump into Sam in the hall on my way out. I greet her and say, "I was wondering if you'd like to take a trip down the Kangamangus with me on Monday, without your two body-guards."

"They're not my bodyguards. I can take care of myself just fine. Besides, how do I know you're not a serial killer?"

"Well, you could ask my ex-wives but they're all dead."

Her face finally cracks a smile and she accepts. I tell her

I'll meet her at nine o'clock Monday morning.

I walk to Weirs in case I have too much to drink. The whole half-mile and drive-in are packed with tents, filled with everything a biker could ever want. There are makeshift tattoo parlors, leather shops, and a hodgepodge of motorcycle accessories. The biggest attraction is the beer tent and it is filled to capacity. Coors is sponsoring the tent this year and they are nice enough to bring the biker girls. For $2.50 you get a 16 oz beer and are able to ogle at their ample breasts. They have standard biker music playing from some crappy band. They are also Camel girls circling the tent handing out smokes.

I want to stay in the tent all night but a poster for pudding-wrestling catches my eye. It is at the Paradise lounge up the strip. The poster doesn't do it justice. Most of the contestants are inhumanly ugly. One of the first two contestants is a 90-pound bone-rack with two teeth. She is pitted against Kong, whose layers of lard hang over her leotard almost waxing the floor. Everyone is screaming for no-teeth but the slow-moving Kong is my favorite. The match lasts about two minutes and ends when the chunky one smothers slim-jim in a wave of flab and pudding. I wave my fist in the air and let out a big howl when my contestant wins. So does Kong. Her armpits are much hairier than mine. Contestant after contestant goes down to my favorite hairy behemoth.

In the final match, she is pitted against a ringer. As lard-o makes her plunge, the eventual winner dodges her and leaps on her ample back. There is a quick count by the referee and Kong is gone. Everybody is yelling, "fixed fight," but the decision is done and so is my evening.

I HEAD TO LEO'S the next morning. He hasn't changed much. He has a team of sled dogs, a brood of kids, and his wife, Katrina, is as nice as ever. Leo made his fortune building birdhouses. When that gets slow he does a little amethyst mining. He has become very comfortable as a Mainer. We have been out of touch for so long that there isn't much for us to talk about. His kids are still young so they are the center of his universe. My developing reality doesn't bring much to the conversation. When I leave, I think about the days when I had been consumed by my little bastards. As much as I hate to admit it, I miss them.

SAM AND I leave the next morning for the Kangamangus. This is the best day so far. The sun is out and the temperature is supposed to hit sixty-five. We skirt the lake heading west until we hit Route 93. It is an hour ride up the highway to Look Mountain, which is where the Kangamangus begins. We stop at a grocery store just off 93 to pack up a lunch for the afternoon. We grab coffee and sit outside on a bench for about half an hour.

"How many Bike Weeks have you been to?" I probe.

"This is my second, I came three years ago with my ex-husband."

"How was that?"

"Not very good, that's why he's my ex."

"No, I meant how was Bike Week."

Sam smiles and says, "The first one is always fun because you don't know what to expect. Is this your first?"

"No, I've been married a couple of times."

She laughs. "Your first Bike Week, shithead."

"Yeah, I just bought my bike this spring after a long hiatus."

"Why'd you stop riding?" she asks.

"Kids, college, house payments, business, all the usual excuses."

Resurrection

"So what brought you back?"

"Timing, discontent, and a gypsy woman."

"Timing and discontent I can understand, but who is the gypsy woman?"

"On the northern coast of Massachusetts there's a little run-down beach resort called Salisbury. It's sort of been my second home since I was a kid. The gypsy woman resides there, and for a few shekels she'll answer any question you have. She gave me the go ahead for my latest journey."

I can tell Sam is starting to get curiously nervous so I back-peddle a little bit. "Maybe we should go back to timing and discontent so I don't sound like a lunatic. I bought my bike, sold my business, kissed my kids goodbye, and let my wife run off with a professor, all in about four months. The timing was perfect. If I didn't do it now, I would be some old fool that would need help getting on his bike. My business was consuming me, the wife I loved was slowly fading away to her self-discovery. My time and my trip had to be. The personal discontent I felt just helped it along."

"That sounds pretty serious," Sam responds.

"Not anymore, my trip is still ahead of me." Even though she seems happy just asking questions, I know it's time to shut up and listen to her. I think that she's going to be real hard to crack. "Okay, now that you've made my heart bleed, what's your story?"

"No kids, no husband, no problems."

"Nothing's that simple."

"I was a horse-trainer until last week when my boss's new wife took my place. Between losing my husband and losing my job I really needed this week away. My friend Jeannie invited me to come with them. She and Will are great. I do kind of feel like an intruder in their room, though."

131

"You look like a horse-trainer."

"Thanks a lot. Do I get a bail of hay and some oats now?"

"Hey, that's a compliment. Your body is strong and athletic. You look like you could wrestle a horse."

"Jesus, you're quite a romantic."

"Well, let's just say I won't be put out to stud anytime soon." I change the subject and ask where she lives.

"I live in Rutland. After I left my husband I moved back in with my mother."

"How long have you been divorced?" I ask.

"Not long enough, it'll be a year next month."

"Was it messy?"

"Yeah, the motherfucker knocked up a friend of mine. I'd say that's messy."

I groan and say, "That's grim. My first wife screwed around a lot. It can really knock you down for a while."

"Well, I'm just starting to pick myself back up. This is the first time I've been on the bike since the divorce."

"The way you ride it looks like you haven't forgotten much. Just out of curiosity, do you always wear a helmet?"

"Always," she replies. "Do you ever wear a helmet?"

"Never, it's like wearing a rubber."

"Yeah, I prefer bareback myself."

Petrified that I might screw up our perfect conversation, I ask her if she wants to continue on. We travel for half an hour as the road cuts through the mountains. We stop at a set of rapids for lunch.

"You know, this would be a nice place to puff one up," I say before we start eating.

"I'm all for that but I don't have any weed."

"Don't worry, I keep all sorts of trinkets in my bike, I'm sure I have some in there."

I had her roll up a fat boy and explain that I always sucked at rolling joints. She is more than happy to oblige with her nimble fingers. After we get a good buzz, we break out lunch and wolf everything down like a couple of teenagers. If there had been a Twinkie left, we would have fought over it.

The sun is at its peak and we are now stripped down to our T-shirts, using our leathers for pillows. We lay there for about an hour not saying much but enjoying the moment. Then that nagging question starts popping up. If I don't make a move Sam's going to think I'm a lame-o, but if I do, I might get shot right down. This dilemma has stumped men for ages. When do you get in the batter's box? I always say immediately, that way if you get thrown out you can always find someone else.

I turn toward her and realize that she's now half-asleep with her back toward me. All I can think about is pulling her big pigtail or giving her a good slap on her fine rump. Instead I decide to attack on the neck by giving her a firm massage and tossing the ball in her court. After about a minute, she starts "umming." She slowly turns over and I feel that success is now imminent.

Reaching over to kiss one another, two little kids come running over our sunning rock scaring the shit out of us. We both start laughing as the tension disappears. The kids take off like they are in trouble and we are left alone for our first kiss.

We spin our way through the final part of the Kangamangus and I believe that we both feel a measure of success. An hour of hard driving has us back at the Naswa. We are both a little tuckered from our long ride and all of the contortions that go along with the game of pursuit.

We decide to toast our good ride at the Tiki bar down at the beach which is now open. The good weather has dragged everybody out. Everyone is half-naked and smiling. Will and

Jeannie have obviously been there for most of the afternoon, he's mumbling and she's stumbling but they're happy to see us.

Will immediately opens his big yap and says, "Here comes the happy couple." This doesn't bother me but Sam gets all red-faced. Jeannie quickly jumps in and swoops her away to escape from Will's liquor-induced needling. While they were at the bar buying another round Will keeps going.

"Thanks for taking her out for the day, I hadn't gotten laid in a week."

"Hey, it was my pleasure," I say with a wide grin.

Will gives me a skeptical look and says, "You're shitting me. You haven't jumped her already."

Being the type of guy I am I let Will's imagination go wherever it wants and say nothing. Will is just about ready to give me a "thataboy" when the girls return. Will gives me the nod that telepathically says, "Don't worry, this is our little secret."

Jeannie asks, "Did you enjoy your trip?" as if she doesn't already have a play-by-play from Sam.

I reply, "It was great. The scenery, weed, and company were all beautiful."

Sam looks embarrassed again like a kid caught getting her first kiss. It's funny because outwardly she seems so tough. She must have adopted this posture as a protective device. The most sensitive of people often wear a mean mask.

With each minute that passes I learn more and more about Sam. The early summer wind changes and it starts to get chilly. Sam and Jeannie go up to their room to put on some more clothes.

Will, now totally stewed, gives me the lowdown on Sam. "Listen, Ian, Sam's been knocked around a lot lately, it seems that every man she gets close to lets her down. I'm her friend. She helped my Jeannie get through her mother's death when no one else would come around. It might not be any of my business but I won't let anyone hurt Sam."

I take into regard that Will's been drinking so rather than answer, I listen.

"Hell, her father was never around, her stepfather raped her, her ex-husband knocked up her friend. Her boss took advantage of her and then fired her. Now you're sniffing around and I don't know shit about you."

As cocked as Will may be I start to get a little hot. "So what's your fucking point?"

"My fucking point is that we really don't know anything about you. You could be just another asshole looking to screw Sam over. So I'm just giving you fair warning that if you fuck with Sam, you fuck with me," Will says with his finger pointing at my chest.

"You know, Will, the way I look at it, Sam and I are none of your fucking business. I've spent most of my life being told what to do between customers, wives, and my business. In fact, the only reason I'm here is so dipshits like you *can't* tell me what to do."

Will obviously isn't impressed by my speech. He quickly jumps up, knocking over his chair, his drink, and just about everything else on the table. He reaches over and grabs me by the shirt and I retaliated by doing the same to him. We proceed to grab, tug, and swear at one another resembling two middle-aged biker ballerinas performing the dance of the egos. The fact is that Will is too drunk to fight and I am too sober. The crowd separates us just as Jeannie and Sam are heading up the beach toward us. Jeannie runs toward Will while Sam stands there dumbfounded.

"Will, what the hell is going on?" Jeannie demands.

Will says, "This asshole, Ian, developed an attitude when

I told him that he better be nice to Sam."

"What the hell are you talking about?" Jeannie asks.

Before Will starts telling too tall of a tale, I chime in. "I'm going to tell you what I told Will. Sam can look out for herself, I don't need a boozed-up babysitter getting involved."

Now Jeannie gets pissed. "Don't talk to me like that."

"It's too fucking late now, isn't it?" I taunt.

Will starts toward me again but is now stopped by Sam and Jeannie. Apparently everyone has chosen their side and I'm standing alone. I figure now is a good time to take a break seeing I've pissed off most of Vermont.

As I am walking back to my room I can still hear Will and Jeannie yapping at me. If I had taken a different attitude, I probably would have been screwing Sam in no time. This is a good sign. My days of appeasement are over.

TUESDAY the weather is miserable but my mood is excellent. I had had so much fun the day before getting under Will's skin. I hadn't heard from Sam so I figure that we're done. It's too bad because Sam had that horse thing going on. I always liked those riding pants plus any girl that rides a lot is usually a bucking bronco in bed.

Rather than sit around and lament my lost lay, I decide to go visit my friend Art. He shouldn't be too busy because of the lousy weather.

The makeshift tent city in the parking lot of the drive-in movie theatre is set up like a big shopping mall with the beer tent as the nucleus. Art has just arrived for the day and his mood isn't good. Art sells higher end handmade leathers and his business at Bike Week depends on good weather to loosen up the wallets of the customers.

I receive his usual sarcastic greeting. "Like the day wasn't grim enough, now I see your ugly face."

"Thanks, Sunshine, it's good to see you too."

Art says, "You know how it is, on a day like this it isn't even worth the effort."

"Don't get suicidal, the weather's supposed to break tomorrow. If it makes you feel any better, I'll buy you a cup of coffee."

I go down to one of the many empty chuck wagons to get our coffees. When I get back, Art is already hard at work giving some twenty-year old juiced-up biker his story of leather.

Art says, "These leathers are all hand-sewn, the hide is strictly American. Pick up this jacket, try it on and tell me if you can't feel the quality."

The anabolic asshole starts trying to nickel and dime Art but he is in no mood for haggling. "Look, if you want to buy a fucking jacket that will fall off you the minute it starts raining, there's a shitload of places that sell that cheap Chinese crap. I don't." Art now puts that look on his face that says, "screw you." It's not because he's nasty or a poor salesman. It's because what he sells, to him, is fine art. No one should ever go into Art's gallery trying to be a critic.

I smirk and say, "Art, congratulations on your graduation from the Dale Carnegie School of Sales."

"Look, I've been doing this a lot of years and I knew that shithead wasn't going to buy anything. He was just a Saturday nighter."

"I'll bite," I say. "What's a Saturday nighter?"

"Every Saturday night when the weather's perfect, the juiced-up muscleheads take their overpriced show bikes for a trip down Main Street. Then it's back to the weight room for more posing. Their idea of a hard ride is a trip to Dunkin' Donuts."

"There does seem to be a lot of them up here, though."

"Yeah, this is their showcase now." Art would know, he's been hitting Laconia and Daytona, selling for the last twenty years. During that time, he's seen every freak, phony, and outlaw biker that those venues serve up. Since I've been absent all those years, Art acts as my encyclopedia, letting me get a taste of what I've missed.

I spent the rest of the day with Art, listening to him tell tales tall and small. I bought him dinner that night and promised to catch up with him at the end of the summer. Art gave me a skullcap for the rest of the trip, telling me that a bald bastard like myself would appreciate it come mid-summer. He also told me that he wished he could come with me. I think life still owes Art one more long ride, just not at this point in time.

As PREDICTED, the weather breaks the next morning. I am anxious to head downtown to see the early arrivals for the upcoming weekend. As I am about ready to hop on my bike I hear a familiar voice.

"Where the hell are you going, Conan?" Sam says.

"I'm heading down to the strip to see all of the road warriors pulling in. The police are out in full force. All the Angels are here and Devil's Disciples have threatened to make a show. If all hell breaks loose, I want to be there."

"Speaking about hell breaking loose, that was a pretty good show yesterday."

I shrug and say, "Yeah, things got a little out of hand. But Will was giving me a boatload of shit."

"He was wasted and he can be a little protective."

"That's cool with me, as far as I'm concerned everything is over. Actually, I kind of enjoyed it."

"Yeah, you would. So you heading out now?" Sam asks.

"I was."

"Can you give me five minutes?"

"For what?"

"Well, I was thinking I might go with you."

"Without your watchdogs, I hope."

"No, I'll muzzle the mutts today."

"Then take your time, I'm not going anywhere."

As I sit there waiting, I think, this is probably a mistake but it might be a fun one. I am not disappointed. Sam comes around the corner and the usual long-sleeved T-shirt is replaced by a little black lace number, one size too tight with no bra so her nips are in full salute. The bottom half of the package is equally as delicious. A snug pair of leather pants shows off an ass that has been riding more than horses. Her outfit is completed by high-heeled, black Tony Llamas that seem to add an inch or two to her height. The total package is adding an inch or two elsewhere. I have now forgotten all of my misgivings about continuing on with Sam.

"Did Jeannie and Will let you go out like that?"

"You are a shithead. Are you ready to go?"

When Sam gets on her bike I realize that she isn't wearing her helmet. Rather than take a chance at poking fun, I keep my mouth shut. She takes the lead pulling out of Naswa with her Swiss Miss pigtail flapping in the wind.

Unfortunately, the Devil's Disciples don't show but it was a perfect day to observe. As the afternoon wears on, Sam and I slowly let down our guard. Our sharp-tongued conversations are replaced by playful chitchat. By the time we hit the beer tent late in the afternoon we are enjoying a lot more physical contact. It started as slow brushes against one another and gradually escalated throughout the day. By the time we had a few coldies, she is sitting in my lap. It took all I had not to disrobe her right there.

The buzz around the beer tent was that the wet T-shirt contest at the Paradise will be a must-see. Sam is up for it although she says she won't participate. Between the suds and the sun, we decide to take a break from one another till that night.

SAM AND I meet in the lobby of the Naswa at eight that evening. We grab a bite at the Mexican restaurant next to the Paradise. Her outfit hasn't changed and her attitude is better than ever. There is no way I am going to be denied tonight.

After we finish dinner, we beeline it to the Paradise because the crowd is backed up to get in. The contest is already underway as we enter and there is no doubt that the talent level is much higher than the pudding wrestling earlier in the week. There are no hairy beasts in this contest and thankfully, Kong stayed home. Most of the contestants are blonde and surgically enhanced. While the crowd is mostly male, there is a couple's corner off to the side of the stage. It makes a great observation post without having to get knocked around by the beer-guzzling knuckle-draggers.

As the night wears on, the contestant's breasts seem to get bigger. The beer that was flowing pretty freely before is now in full chugging stage. The noise level cancels out the hard rock that plays for each contestant. Everything seems on the edge of being out of control.

Sam takes leave to go to the ladies room and has to tunnel her way through the wild horde of party-goers. I keep only half an eye out for her knowing that the crowd is in a pretty good mood. When she is just about back to our nook, I see her stall on the floor and start getting into a high-test argument with some guy. I hesitate for one second thinking, man, this woman's a lot of trouble.

By the time I reach her, this guy is so pissed that it looks like he's going to whack her. I reach over and grab his shoulder, pulling him away from her. This gives him the perfect opportunity to hit me full flush with an excellent right hand. My knees knock but I stay upright long enough to get tangled up with my new admirer. It is all so quick that I don't even get a chance to look at the guy that I am now attacking. I don't get to see what Sam is doing, either, because two big-ass bouncers have dragged us out to the sidewalk. The next thing I know, my friend and I are in the police wagon, hand-cuffed next to each other. We don't really talk much on the way to the Hotel Laconia but as much as I could gather this is the shithead that had been married to Sam.

The hotel is extremely busy that evening with DWIs, assaults, and drunk and disorderlys. I don't get much sleep between people puking and yelling about not receiving their rights. Even though I have left my old life only five days ago, I am making great strides in my new one. I'm stuck in jail, but I can post bail tomorrow. When I was stuck at the Honey Bee that was a life-long prison sentence.

THE NEXT MORNING I have to pay a hundred dollar fine for drunk and disorderly along with about fifty of my comrades. It has been twenty-four hours since I have gotten any sleep and I am looking forward to a shower and a bed. That is until I see Sam. She is leaning against her motorcycle outside the station and before I can get a word out she starts apologizing as if what has happened is her fault.

"I'm sure you're not in the mood to talk to me," she started, "but I'm awful sorry about last night. I'm sure you know by now that that was my ex. I should have just walked away from him. Is there any way I can make it up to you?"

"Yeah, there is, but I'll get to that in a minute. First, answer me one question. How is it that I can get in so much trouble in such a short period of time with just one woman? Every time I turn around someone wants to kick my ass just because I'm sniffing around you. Is there anybody else I should know about that wants to pummel me?"

Thinking I am pissed off, Sam looks defensive. I think it's time to let her off the hook.

I continue, "If I had the chance to do this week over again I wouldn't change a thing, not even last night. I'm having the time of my life."

"I don't get you."

"For years, my life had been the same day to day, banging my head against a brick wall and doing a slow bleed. Since I bumped into you at least nothing's been predictable. Our first date went so good your friends wanted to beat me up. Then when I figured I was on the verge of getting laid, I end up in jail. I'm just curious what will be next, but I definitely want to find out. That's the reason I came up here. My life is now exciting. And to answer your first question, there is a way you can make it up to me. Let's have some savage sex."

"That sounds serious."

"Not at all. Sex shouldn't be serious, that's for all the drones who barely enjoy it. When I say savage sex, it's an adventure. You can't control it and you never know where it's going to end up. It's loud, hot, wet, romantic, and honest. It might even be good."

"I hope you don't use that line on other girls you meet."

"Not for a very long time." Sam offers me a ride back to the motel. Driving back I can't help but remember that long ago summer day with Lisa when I first learned that sex in its purest form can be an ultimate high and not a mere procreative act.

I wonder what Sam would be like. Could her pleasure be kinky or common? Is she a gurgler or a gulper? Is she like the rain forest or the Sahara?

We pull up to the motel and stand there for a minute like two gunslingers waiting to see who would make the first move. I blink and give her a kiss and then admit that a little sleep may be just what I need. She has to catch up on her laundry and do some shopping. Sam says she will come wake me up later that afternoon. I give her my key and we go off in different directions once again. I wonder what will stop us from making love this time?

I'm actually glad Sam gave me some space. If I went right to bed with her, I'd end up going to la-la land the minute after I dropped my load. Age has slowed me down a bit. It now takes me a while longer to restart chubby after his first go round. On the good side, the first one can last as long as I want. Years ago I was the fastest gun in the West but I could keep shooting all day. Now I try and make the first shot count because my gun takes time to reload. Other than that not much has changed, especially my imagination.

Halfway through my hot shower Mr. Imagination was working perfectly so I squeezed off a quickie before hitting the hay. Usually I twist and turn a couple of times when I'm dancing with the sandman but not today. I was in deep space.

I eventually come to, not awakened by the roar of an unmuffled bad boy or a chambermaid vacuuming the hallway. It is a smell that moves my eyelids open. The fragrance isn't overpowering or bottled. I slowly leave my trance to discover that it is the smell of Sam that has gotten my Alpha attention. The visual is equally as alluring, a sliver of late day sun acts as a muted spotlight. Sam's well-cut body is visible through a black fishnet tank top and matching panties. I am hooked before my eyes are fully open. I am at full salute but I stay under the covers to play dead so she can take the lead. I do a slow roll to let her know that I am stirring. She comes over and sits on the edge of the bed and gently begins to rub my neck and shoulder blades. She kisses my neck and asks me if I have any protection. Still drowsy I say, "I have a .22 pistol in my saddlebags."

Sam quietly says, "That's good, do you plan on shooting me after you get laid?"

We both start laughing as she falls into bed. Now we don't care. We slowly start inspecting each other with our hands as the kisses become more pronounced. Sam whispers that she had been thinking about our savage sex conversation while she had been in the shower. "I realized with the other men I have been with that we never really talked about sex, we danced around it or we joked about it but we were never honest about it."

Fearing Sam might be thinking too much, I throw it back in her court. "Let's not have a good conversation ruin good sex. Take what you need. Be yourself, please yourself. That's about as honest as you can be."

I quickly start to kiss her passionately in order to stop her soul searching. Sam obliges and we ever so slowly begin to taste each other. We are like explorers making our way to our objective but making enlightening discoveries as we take each step. Sam is full of surprises. While her exterior looks strong, she shows a softness in bed. It seems like she is finally letting down her guard.

Sam's breasts are not large but they have a beautiful firm shape that sweeps upward. Her nipples are the finishing touch. Caressed and sucked, they are like little rockets—you could hang your jacket on them. Working my way down, the rest of Sam is pure delight. Her belly is soft and adorned by a ring in her little button. Nibbling her jewel, I can start to feel that minor tremble over Sam's body and a small earthquake erupted as the nibbling headed south.

Before dining at the Y, I take my own advice and remember that I have neglected the other half of her body. I start over at her feet and again begin my slow crawl to her heaven. Taking this route is a stroke of genius. It's a road seldom taken in sex and the view is spectacular. Sam's feet are small, her legs are strong and perfectly defined. She teases me by giving me a view of her warming herself up. To my delight, Sam is my first Mexican hairless. While I recently poked fun at the Chihuahuas at the Golden Banana, confronted with Sam's hairless honey pot I am more than ready for the new experience.

Sam does a slow but controlled roll to offer me another scenic vista. She is now on all fours tempting me with her best asset, a tight round rump that yearns for attention. I take my massage up to her thighs and ass and painstakingly work them over, trying not to miss anything. Sam now has herself well on her way as I finally work my way into my late lunch. Dining is divine, the dish I am devouring is wickedly wet. The shaven view exposed a love button that is protruding as opposed to being tucked behind love flaps. I go to work and so does Sam. She is a pro-blow and it takes everything I have not to give her a salty shower. While I am happy not to overshoot my desires, Sam has no problem with hers. Informing me that she is coming, I am surprised by the milky bath that she gives me. We take a short intermission to share our discoveries. The sun is going down. We have already been at it for two hours and we are only halfway there.

"Ian, you could have come if you wanted to, I know I almost had you there."

"I'll save that for dessert. Speaking of dessert, you don't disguise your orgasms very well."

145

"I know, I sort of come like a guy."

"It's fucking beautiful."

"Thanks."

Sam crawls on top of me and she's drenched. I easily slid into her and she begins her slow ride, holding the top of the bed like reins. Her smiles and sighs increase as she picks up her pace to a trot. She quickly goes into a full gallop and she is sharing her joy like a Comanche warrior. Abruptly she pulls in the reins and rolls over again to her knees, holding onto the bed. I can't help but get one more taste. I start at the base of her back and work my way down, giving her a rim job on the way. Sam not only doesn't protest but begins to plead for more.

She and I are now at each other's whim. We open up and let it all happen. I let Sam guide me. She wants to be ridden hard in all ways, pausing long enough between each session to relish our accomplishment. Each act we perform has a natural energy. During the unnatural acts, the force reaches its height. I had never thought that there were still things to learn about sex but I was wrong. Every woman is her own world and being invited to play in it is like being a virgin again. My new life will only allow a woman in for short periods of time. I will love them all but I won't stay with any. This is now one of my personal rules.

Sam and I didn't let up until the next morning. When the sun was up, we sat by the lake reliving our escapades like we had known each other forever. There were no promises or regrets although Sam kept beating around the "what's next" question. She never directly asked so I think she's happier not knowing for now.

IT SEEMS LIKE the week has just started and it is already winding down. In only a couple of days, Weirs will be transformed back into another of the small tourist traps that dot the shore of Lake Winnipesaukee. The crowds are now building to a peak for the weekend bike races.

Sam went over to Will and Jeannie's to pick up her bags. I don't recall if I even asked her or not but apparently she is staying with me for the rest of the week. I can't imagine how she can fit all of her crap on one bike. When she comes back to the room to set up camp, she mentions that Will and Jeannie were wondering if we'd like to go to a party down in Meredith. The party is going to be held in a giant barn with a live band and it is only ten minutes down the road. However, I do wonder if Will was just trying to create a second opportunity to give me more grief, especially now that I am tagging his precious little Samantha. I don't really give a shit but I bring it up to Sam anyway.

"Is this Will's chance to cut me down?"

"Aren't you over that yet? He hasn't mentioned it and I don't think he even remembers it."

That night around eight, we meet Will and Jeannie to head over to the party. Will walks over to me and says, "Sorry things got out of hand the other day. I was pretty lit and you know I think a lot of Sam."

Seeing him pull back, I say, "Hey, don't worry about it. I was being a shithead, too. So how'd you hear about this party?"

"These guys have it every year, they live in Meredith. It's usually pretty peaceful, there's no gangs, just old fucks like us. The music's always great, too. They charge ten bucks to cover the band and beer."

"Sounds good, you guys go ahead and we'll follow."

There is a dirt road about a half-mile long that leads up to the barn. Bikes are already parked single file along the road. We can hear the music as we stroll up to the barn. Surprisingly enough, it isn't the Bob Seger/Steppenwolf crap that I had expected. It is more rock-a-billy, it sounds like my man Sleepy La

Beef. Sleepy made his bones playing around the Boston area in venues like the Blue Star and the notorious Hillbilly Ranch. He plays perfect party music.

The barn, set on top of a knoll, has its doors open. The crowd spills out onto the lawn where a beer tent is set up. We pay our ten dollars at a roped off table and head toward the dozen or so kegs. Will and Jeannie stay by the tent while Sam and I cruise around the crowd, looking at all of the sights.

The inside of the barn acts as a dancehall. While I am in full party mode, Sam seems a little pensive. Rather than screw up a good night, I figure I'll just let her be. Strangely enough, I bump into an old schoolmate from Gloucester that I haven't seen in years. Joe grew up in a fishing family and inherited a boat right at the time when the fishing industry was falling apart. While the fishing sucked, Joe seemed to prosper. No one could figure it out but Joe was a guy that everyone liked. I think people just assumed that he was a damned good fisherman. That was until the day that Joe got bagged for smuggling.

"Joe, long time no see."

"Duke, my brother, what's happening?"

"I'm up here living the life of a rebel, drinking beers, riding my bike. This is my friend, Samantha."

"Sam, how'd you hook up with this loser?"

"It was a Bike Week mistake," Sam says flatly.

I give her the hairy eyeball and then turn back to Joe. "What's been happening with you? The last time I heard, you were vacationing in Danbury."

"Yeah, they got everything—the house, the boat, and the wife. Now I sell cellular phones to punks. You still in the restaurant business?"

"No, I just sold my last one and that's it for me."

Joe and I suck up a beer together and relive old times before he goes off to track down his friends. Sam still has that sour look on her face and I can't take it anymore. Against my better judgment, I ask her what is wrong.

"Nothing," she answers. This is the kind of "nothing" that I know means something.

Probing her, I say, "Nothing except?"

"The week's just going by too fast."

"It's not over yet," I say, trying to pacify her. I don't know why but I get the feeling that there could be more trouble with Sam. She has that "are you going to call me in the morning?" look.

Although the conversation is going in the wrong direction, the night takes a turn for the better when Sam and I cut out of the party early. We go back to Naswa and start to replay our antics from the night before.

THE NEXT morning is the start of the bike races. We head to the track around ten. The preliminaries have already started. The crowd seems a little more upscale than my friends at Weirs. Maybe it is because the New Hampshire International Speedway has become one of the places to be seen. The races themselves are a lot like Nascar, slick and predictable. There are no more dirt tracks or Harleys and Indians chasing one another in some monumental battle for motorcycle superiority. Today's races are like an Oriental showcase for Hondas and Kawasakis. After a couple of hours, my disinterest in the races is obvious, as is Sam's. We decide that a good hard ride might clear out the cobwebs. As much as I want to go, I can feel the tension that had started last night coming to a head.

We decide to take a cruise to White Mountain National Forest. There's a little campsite at the base of Mt. Washington that we pull into. The site is empty and we decide to set up camp there for a while. I take a quick trip to the general store down the street to pick up lunch, a bottle of wine, and some firewood.

By the time I get back Sam has played house. She has dragged over a picnic table and a blanket is laid out next to where we will build a fire. Her jacket serves as a pillow. The whole scene is a little too domestic. We are all by ourselves, laid out before the big mountain. The fire is taking the chill out of the air. We are sitting there enjoying the wine and staring into the flames.

"Ian, what are your plans after tomorrow?" she asks softly.

"As crazy as it sounds, I have no firm plans, all I know is that the summer is mine. I just plan on pointing my bike north and seeing where it takes me."

"Sounds romantic but it's probably a hard way to live."

"Sometimes the hardest things are the best for you. What I've done is give myself another chance at life. I've had a house, a wife, cars, kids, success, and also failure. None of those things satisfied me. That world wasn't bad for me but it was never right for me, either."

"A lot of people feel like that. I feel like that."

"Yeah, but unlike most people, I've acted on those feelings."

I see Sam absorb all that she has heard. We stare at each other without blinking.

"So what's Samantha's future look like?" I ask, turning the tables.

"It can only get better from here. Right now I have nothing to go back to. I have no job, and I'm living with my mom. All I have are bad memories that I'm trying to shake. This weekend has really helped but I just don't know if I want to go back."

"Well, maybe you shouldn't."

"What else would I do?"

"Ride with me for a little while. Maybe it'll give you time to figure out what you want before you go home."

I can see Sam questioning herself and the offer. I continue, "Listen Sam, it wouldn't be forever. You can leave whenever you want, it will only be for as long as you need. You might even enjoy it."

"Sounds like a good offer, it's not like I have anything to lose."

"There's only one thing you have to understand. I don't want to get attached."

Sam nods and says, "I can live with that."

Before we drive back later that afternoon, we pay homage to Mt. Washington by making love in its shadow. When we get back to Weirs, we take a couple of runs up and down the strip with our brothers as a show of respect for the week we had.

As I fall asleep that night with Sam, I wonder if Emily is sharing her bed with the Professor.

The next morning we pack for our voyage. Before we leave, Sam goes to say goodbye to Will and Jeannie. I have time to reflect on the week that has been the beginning of my resurrection.

As Sam and I pull out of town, I know I have a long way to go but I can't wipe the grin off my face thinking of how far I have already come and how much fun it has been.

Chapter 4: Soul Mining

I WAS GLAD TO LEAVE Laconia. Bike Week is like Las Vegas, as fun as it is, it's not reality. Sam and I headed to Portsmouth because I wanted to get some more hieroglyphics. From there, we planned to travel up the coast of Maine.

As we got closer to Portsmouth, the long parade of bikes going home started to weed out. For the last week we had ruled the road. The longer we rode, the more we realized that the automobile was back in charge. We were once again the hunted on the open road. I was curious to see how Sam would react to roughing it. Although I still had plenty of cash left over, my plan was to learn to survive on the road once again. The rest of the trip wasn't meant to be a vacation but a lifestyle change.

When we got to Hobo's Tattoo, we found out that my artist Jason was out for a couple of hours. I didn't want anyone else to do the work so Sam and I decided to grab a beer and wait until Jason was available. We walked to the Muddy River and Sam mentioned that it might be nice to walk around town. My mood turned a little sour. I told her to feel free to go and that I'd meet her at the studio in a few hours.

"Aren't you going to be my tour guide?" she asked.

"I just don't feel like it."

"Why? What's the matter?"

"This is my home turf, I'm leaving this area for a reason,

it's too soon to be back here."

Sam caught my drift and went off to browse the shops with the yuppies. I didn't regret my decisions for a minute, but being so close to home I couldn't help but wonder what Emily was up to. I hid in the darkest corner of the River. I didn't want anyone I know to recognize me. Finally, it was time to see Jason.

I had sketched out the first row of hieroglyphics that would stretch from shoulder to shoulder. The symbols simply encapsulated my life before my resurrection. Jason went right to work and about an hour into it Sam showed up. Sam was intrigued by Jason's slow, meticulous work but she seemed confused about my choice of body art. When Jason finished and bandaged me up, I had had enough of Portsmouth. I wouldn't repeat my mistake until the end of the summer when I would receive my second row.

We jumped on U.S. Route 1 and went north with the intention of skirting the entire Maine coast in the coming weeks. The day was already blown so we looked for a campground where we could set up for a day or two. Kennebunk was about an hour up and there was a campground right by the ocean. We pulled in at about six o'clock and went to get supplies for the next couple days.

The sun was just about down by the time we had the fire lit. The night air was cold so we put one of our sleeping bags next to the fire. As I was coming back from our pee tree, I noticed Sam had an eerie presence in the firelight. It struck me then how little I actually knew about Sam. Will had told me that she had a rough life but Sam hid her secrets well. I wonder what it would take to get her to open up. Maybe some marijuana would relax her. I went over to my bike and rolled up a fatty. Back at the fire I grabbed a twig to spark it up. As the weed launched us into dreamland, I decided to take a shot at interrogating Sam.

"Tell me about Rutland. Did you grow up there?"

"No, I grew up in Plattsburg, New York, on the other side of Lake Champlain."

"It's cold as hell there, isn't it?"

"Yeah, it's a hell hole," she said softly.

"So how did you end up in Rutland?"

"What is this, twenty questions?"

"No, but the fact is, I don't know that much about you. You could be Lizzie Borden for all I know."

"What you don't know can't hurt you."

"Cut it out. Do you think you're the only one that's ever been kicked around?"

"Stop being an asshole."

"An asshole wouldn't be asking. Come on, your life couldn't have been that bad. What's the matter, Mommy wouldn't buy you the Barbie doll?"

I now witnessed a different side of Sam. Her face said it all. She wasn't just mad, she was wounded.

"You need to know about my misery? Think about a little girl growing up without a father. She never even knew him. This girl's mother falls in love and marries another man who seems affectionate and hard working. This monster gains the trust of the little girl by manipulating her longing to be loved into a sick nightmare. By the end of her first year of high school, she is pregnant with her stepfather's child. The girl is so young that she doesn't even realize it until a visit to the doctor brings everything out in the open. At first, her mother doesn't want to believe the truth, then she finds a way to blame the girl to protect her own demented world. The stepfather goes to jail. The mother is shamed. The mother and daughter move far enough away to start over. The baby is given up for adoption and the young girl is supposed to just go on like it never happened. As this girl becomes a woman, she keeps falling for men that resemble the stepfather who wronged her. She longs for a man that will take care of her. Instead they use her and her insecurities to just pile on more damage to a woman who now wonders if there is anything good left in her world. That girl is me. Did you enjoy listening to me bleed one more time? Is your curiosity satisfied? The reason I'm here is to get a chance to forgive myself. I don't need you to heal me, just be my friend."

I learned more about Sam in ten minutes by the fire than I knew about any of my wives. I'm never speechless but there was nothing left to ask Sam. She just sat there trembling with energy. The flames flickered against her face, which now looked pained. I didn't say a word the rest of the night.

THE NEXT morning I realized how old I was. Camping out used to be a joyful pursuit, now it just seems to be a lot of work. The ground was harder than I remember, every bone in my body made a funny crack when I rolled out of my bag. Where was my warm shower? There was no coffee. The only bathroom available I had to share with either animals or strangers. Every nuance of being clean, fed, and happy was a challenge.

Sam's mood was much better this morning. She didn't seem to suffer from the aftereffects of our conversation or a night of sleeping on hard ground. By the time we got ourselves together, we could tell it was going to be a hot day. We decided that the beach was in order.

We took a short ride to York. Neither one of us had bathing suits so we hit one of the tacky, seasonal beach stores to attempt to find something to wear that wasn't too repulsive. I chose floral baggies that made me look like a reject from a Jimmy

Buffet concert. Sam decided on a slick two-piece lycra Speedo. I told her that she looked great but she didn't believe me. We both picked outfits that we never would have worn if we were at home. We bought a cheap mat to throw on the sand and Sam assumed the position of being a sun goddess.

Although I love the sun, my makeup wouldn't allow me to lie on the beach for a minute. So while Sam worked on her tan, I took my Raybans and my new ugly shorts and walked the length of the beach. The water was nut cracking cold so there would be no quick dips. The scenery was excellent. I was like a peeping tom behind my shades. School was out and the beach was littered with jailbait. I don't recall girls looking like that when I was young enough to be legal. When I got to the end of the beach, I perched myself on some rocks that made a perfect gawking point.

I noticed one particular young girl that looked a lot like Sam. She seemed to be so free and happy. She was with her friends circling in and out of the frigid waters. For her, there seemed to be no worries, only a simple celebration of her joyous youth. Looking at that girl, I could only imagine what Sam went through at that age. I wonder what kind of freak would ruin someone that young and innocent. What goes through their mind? Is it a need for power and control or just some perverse pleasure? Whatever the story, there is no redemption. Sam could never be the same as that girl frolicking in the water. I wonder how long the bastard was in jail. It probably wasn't long enough. Could he be putting some other young girl through that torture once again? That prick deserves to die for what he did, but in the real world there is no justice for people like Sam. Today's world only offers us excuses for their behavior.

As pissed off as I am thinking about what Sam's stepfather did, I have to look at my struggles with my own manipulation of women. I am more cunning than an abuser. While my prey is at least close to my age, my technique is especially despicable. I learn everything I can about a woman and put it all in a mental diary to be processed and used for my own satisfaction. There was no reason I had to drag Sam's secrets out of her last night. I already knew half of the story from her friends, Will and Jeannie. What purpose did it serve to have her relive it? While there is nothing illegal about my tendencies, I question whether I am better than any other abuser.

As I head back down the beach, I figure I have done enough soul searching. I do feel like I owe Sam some respect. Maybe the best way to show her would be to relax and enjoy our short time together this summer. My reason for bringing Sam along was purely lust. Apparently this has changed.

As I approach, the fair-skinned biker babe is now getting fried.

"Hey Sam, you look like a lobster."

"Yeah, I think I've had enough sun."

"Would Samantha like to go play for the rest of the day?"

"Where do we start?"

"Let's walk downtown, I must play some skeeball."

"That game's for geeks."

"No, that game is not for geeks. A truly great game of skeeball is an art form. It's not about putting the ball in the highest-numbered circle, it's about coupons. If you score a lot of points, you get a lot of coupons. Those coupons are redeemable for merchandise. I succeed when I have more coupons than the little bastards around me. After ten dollars worth of games, I always count my tickets. This tells me if my skeeball proficiency is still up to snuff. When I'm finished I go over to the prize counter to see what my tickets will buy me. It's never enough for the transistor radio so rather than save up my tickets I give them to the kid who looks like he really needs them. Although those tickets don't mean anything to me, the kid I give them to always treats them like gold. Maybe the kid just hangs around there all day waiting for saps like me to give them tickets. I'll probably see the little shit walking down the street with my transistor radio some day."

Sam gives me a look like I've lost all of my marbles and says, "You're a worse geek than I thought but let's go down-town anyway. Maybe I can show you a different path and intro-duce you to air hockey."

The first must-stop was Goldenrods, an old-fashioned candy store/soda fountain. Sam was mesmerized by the giant window that showcased the taffy wheel. She seemed comforted by the slow roll of the machine, like it reminded her of a good time long ago. I think taffy sucks but I bought some for Sam anyway.

After we left Goldenrod's, I brought Sam for a reading from the psychic woman down the street. She was an older woman who was all dolled up in gypsy paraphernalia. Sam seemed open to the reading. We slid into the curtained-off closet.

The old woman gently took Sam's hand and told her, "Your lines tell me that you've been lost but that you will shortly re-turn home and find a lot of the peace that you are looking for. I also see a career change, this will be good for you."

The rest of the five-minute reading was vague enough to apply to almost any woman. Sam seemed intrigued by the things that the psychic got right.

After leaving the old woman, we walked toward a Native American trading post that we passed on the way back to the beach. As we browsed through the Indian goods, Sam said, "That gypsy woman was good, huh?"

"She was okay, but nothing like my gypsy woman back in Salisbury."

"What's so special about her?" Sam inquired.

"She doesn't glance over things, there are no half-truths. My gypsy woman crawls right in your soul. She knows the whole story without speaking a word. She will always give you a yes or no answer and she never leaves you any doubt."

"You really believe in her?"

"I never made a major decision without her. I trust her with my life."

"She sounds creepy."

Sam goes back to her shopping while I am entertained by a book about Northeastern Indian tribes. I was delighted to see a chapter on my friend, Masconomet. Even though I was lost in my book, I did catch Sam making eyes at a beaded Indian belt. I go over and offer to buy the belt for her but she tells me no, it's a little pricey.

"I'd like to buy it for you."

I see she's a little uncomfortable with my offer. "I was just admiring it, I don't need it."

"Cut the crap, it'll look good on you."

Sam protested all the way to the register. The belt cost fifty bucks. To me it was just funny money but Sam acted as if it was a big deal. Maybe she just felt like I was trying to buy her. When we got outside she was still arguing with me. I wondered if Sam was one of those women who gravitated toward men who treated her poorly. My sister Kathryn was like that. Each relationship was progressively worse. If there was a man who treated her well, she couldn't get away from him fast enough. But if the guy was the biggest prick on the planet, she would always run to him. The last bastard she ran to laid her down for good with a shotgun. The good news is that the motherfucker shot himself, too. I hope Sam knows better than my sister.

We went down to the air hockey table where Sam punished me for three games. I then took her over and educated her on the finer points of skeeball.

For some reason, we both seemed to be in full play mode. We took a stroll over to a place called Bogarts for a cold beer. The frosties were great but the menu didn't really cut it. At the campground we had seen a flyer for a seafood joint about five miles from the beach called Lobster in the Ruff.

The front of the restaurant looked like your typical tourist trap but in the back it turned into a full scale clambake, complete with picnic tables, horseshoe pits, and volleyball nets. While the front was littered with Oldsmobiles and Buicks that had tennis balls on each antenna, the back was full of motorcycles and pickups.

The day was getting long in the tooth and the sun had almost evaporated. Sam and I had changed out of our awkward swimsuits back into our middle-aged biker gear. For the next two hours, all we did was drink beer and pig out. Being born and brought up in Essex, I knew how to lead Sam through a proper clambake. We started with chowder and then worked our way into a couple of plates of steamers. Next was lobster and corn on the cob. We threw in side orders of onion rings and scallops to satisfy our cholesterol craving. Sam, being a flatlander, had never had this experience before, at least not a proper one.

The conversation was as good as the food. Even though I was well in my forties and Sam was in her thirties, we talked about our future like two teenagers, like it was all ahead of us. Sam was hoping to settle down and run her own horse farm. She envisioned another man in her future but only one that didn't control the reins. She felt comfortable in Vermont and had no thoughts of moving. She saw no kids in her future. After her first experience, I couldn't blame her.

My future was a lot harsher but easier to accomplish. I see

myself on the road for good, staying in a location just long enough to feel like I belong. That's when I know it's time to leave. My love life will also follow these rules. Maybe I'll work or maybe I'll just become the ultimate road bum. It's hard to think of ever going back to the life I had.

THE NEXT morning we left Kennebunk and continued up the coast. Each stop was its own two-day adventure. We would pull into a campground and take it easy for the first day, scouting out the area. The second day we would take on the location with a full-scale assault on all it had to offer. It seemed that as soon as we set up the tent it was time to take it down.

The stops added up quickly. There was Portland, Sebago Lake, Wiscasset. From Wiscasset we headed over to Fayette to visit my brother. He's a logger and trucker. Over the years he has accumulated quite a lot of properties. Since I hadn't visited him in about fifteen years, he dragged us around to each tract as if it was prized Manhattan real estate. John still dreams big and works hard. Our visit was pretty good but the best part was sleeping in a bed.

After two weeks, camping had become a lot easier. We closed in on Bar Harbor and the weather was treating us fine. We decided to take our time there. We were lucky enough to find a campsite in Arcadia National Park. Cadillac Mountain is its centerpiece and also the highest point in the Atlantic coast. The park is popular for its rock climbing, kayaking, and wildlife.

As pristine as the National Park is, Bar Harbor is equally as phony. If you're too fucking arrogant for the Hamptons, you move up to Bar Harbor. There are a lot of sushi restaurants, chic boutiques, and fags. That bitch Martha Stewart has a place here. I always wanted to screw her.

The campground was mobbed and we were lucky to get a spot. Our site was the size of a postage stamp. It was on the edge of where the tents were separated from the RV's. The uniqueness of the camp was startling. It was a giant rockscape with small twisted spruces that looked like they were trimmed by Pablo Picasso. The ocean is right on the other side of the grounds. The water was extremely clear, cold, and almost a Caribbean blue. Rock cliffs surrounded the waterfront.

Once Sam and I were done setting up, we were anxious to go explore. We were also anxious to get away from our neighbors in the massive Winnebago next to us. They were a family of large, loud, and rude Jerseyites. All they did was scream at one another. Maybe if we left for the day, they would be gone by the time we returned.

We decided to take our bikes to the top of Cadillac Mountain since the day was getting late. Although the mountain is known for its sunrises, the sunset was equally as stunning. The harbor was beneath us and it looked like a miniature city to a train set. Dead west we could see the rolling mountains of Maine that are the tail end of the Appalachian Trail. Sam and I were just sitting there soaking it all in. It dawned on me then that Sam and I were becoming friends. It was an unexpected surprise.

Just as that thought was passing, Sam said, "You know, I've really enjoyed this trip so far. Thanks for asking me along."

"That's funny, I was just thinking about how well this has all turned out."

We stopped on the way back and picked up two bad ass steaks, a bottle of Royal, charcoal, and a stick of bread. We were all ready for a romantic dinner. We had just poured our first glass and had thrown the steaks on the fire when the family from hell returned from their shopping trip. Their two fat kids were screaming for food like they didn't have enough lard to hold them over until Labor Day. Sam and I were quietly praying that Mom would break out the Twinkies. As if the two little shits weren't bad enough, Mom and Dad were having their own brawl. Apparently Pop had flirted with some waitress at Denny's. I could imagine that if this chubby hubby was eyeballing his server, it was because he wanted to throw her on an open spit. His old lady wouldn't let up. Each moment that passed, her voice was raised another octave. I did feel a little bad for her though. Her plight was probably predictable seeing that she was so painfully ugly.

Our quiet dinner now resembled an episode of "The Osbournes." Luckily, when we sat down for our steak, the dinner bell rang at the Frankenstein household and it was actually peaceful. In the quiet of the night, we could faintly hear their chomping and it sounded like hyenas polishing off a carcass in the Serengeti.

Sam and I cozied up next to the fire and just as we were creating our own heat, the puppies were let out of their playpen. Their game was soccer and they took turns using the side of the Winnebago as their goal. Each time there was a score, Mom would give a red flag and tell them that Dad was about to kick their fat asses. After twenty goals and twenty warnings, the two Pugsly's were finally worn out. After a case of Little Debbie's and a glass of whole milk, the neighbors from hell were done for the night.

Before Sam and I got down to some good screwing, I tiptoed over to their campsite and grabbed the soccer ball. With a knife, I peeled it like an apple and carefully placed the pieces back in their yard. Sam looked at me as if I was demented at first, but then the thought of the little pricks waking up and finding the ball hit her and we both cracked up.

It was such a pleasure the next morning to see my two little friends observing the soccer ball spread out around their plot. Mom and Dad came out and played detective. Their theory on the crime was that a wild bear had come around looking for food and had substituted the soccer ball for a meal. This family was starting to become fun if you could stand the racket.

Sam and I decided to rough it that day and climb one of the many trails to the top of Cadillac Mountain. The trail we chose was about four and a half miles long. The path didn't go directly up the mountain but crisscrossed the base before climbing up. Most everything the government spends its money on means nothing, however the investment in these National parks is worth every cent.

The start of the trail shoots you through a natural tunnel that runs through a dense thorny thicket. After a ten-minute walk, you descend to a beautiful lagoon that's surrounded by sunning rocks and cat-o-nine tails. This lagoon serves as an aviary for the hundreds of species of birds that make this area their summer home. From that point you start a corkscrew crawl around the mountain. Each step offers a different view. Seal Island is to your east. The entrance to the harbor is to the north. To the west is the interior of Maine. The south offers you a view of the ragged Maine coast heading toward Portland.

Four and a half miles doesn't seem like much but by the time we reached the peak, we were exhausted. Sam and I were pleased with our accomplishment, we acted like Sir Hillary conquering Mt. Everest. After a long pause at the top, we headed down a different path. The views were pretty much the same except we now saw rock climbers. They were challenging a huge headwall of rock that was carved into the side of the mountain.

We decided we could use a little pampering that evening. We got cleaned up, jumped on the bikes, and went to Bar Harbor to hang with the beautiful people. This ritzy burg offered great people-watching. The women all resembled Jackie O. Their classiness was understated but they reeked of cash. Their suitors wore Izods and khakis. Leather deck shoes were mandatory. Eveningwear consisted of unisex windbreakers with yachting symbols splashed on the sleeves. The car of choice was a Rover but there was a sprinkling of Humvee's, Beamers, and Mercedes.

Sam and I looked very out of place. While we were watching them, they seemed to be mystified by us. We could feel the discomfort when we pulled into an outdoor eatery overlooking the harbor. They gave us that "there goes the neighborhood" look. Sam and I enjoyed playing our role.

Even though the joint was snobby, the food was excellent and the stares that we got were priceless. After dinner we walked through town, hitting all of the expensive shops. We made believe we had enough money to purchase the overpriced crap in the places. Sam was particularly amused when I went into a men's clothing store that specialized in nautical wear. For her entertainment, I pulled together and tried on an outfit consisting of a polo shirt, khaki trousers, a blue belt with little whales on it, and a navy blue jacket with anchor buttons. The shopkeeper was not amused but Sam was.

The night was perfect for a ride so we took a jaunt up north before we headed back to the campground. We landed back at the site at about 10:30 that night. Everything seemed pretty quiet but we could see some waning fires. We pulled into our nook and parked the bikes, looking forward to a fire. Just as we put our machines to rest, we heard a commotion coming from our friends in the Winnebago. Mom and Dad were storming over in our direction. Dad landed right in front of me and proceeded to open his big yap.

"You know, I don't appreciate you disturbing my family with your goddamned choppers."

"Really?" I retorted. "Well, it's the only thing that'll muffle the sound of your two little bastards over there."

I notice my neighbor's flappy jowls clenched tight and his face was the color of a Red Delicious. There was background noise from his wife but the words were indistinguishable. She just sounded like a Pekinese yapping. Dad put his finger right on my chest and said, "I didn't come all the way from Jersey to have my family's vacation ruined by some old fucking biker and his bitch."

I was now so pissed that my face relaxed into a pre-fight grin. Before he could say another word, I leveled that fat fuck. It was funny when he hit the ground, it sounded like a lot of food being sloshed around in a trashcan.

"I'll fucking sue you," he screamed.

I perched myself over his torso and proceeded to give him little dope slaps every time he opened his mouth.

"Tell you what, Fatso, you apologize to Sam and we'll forget this ever happened."

He tried to worm his way out from under me. I wouldn't let him move until he apologized.

"Ian, just forget it, let him go," I hear Sam say from behind me. She was right but I was having too much fun. You run into people like this guy everywhere but you rarely have the opportunity to slap them around. While I'm taking in the joy of the moment, I notice that we now have spectators. All they saw was the tail end of our confrontation that made me look like the bully. On Sam's second request I let him go. His wife was screaming, his kids were crying, and all the spectators were asking him if he was okay. With all the activity, the park manager showed up. He went right over to the family, getting only their side of the story. After about three minutes of talking with Whimpering Willy, he walked over to Sam and myself.

"Pack up your stuff and go," he told us.

"We're leaving but this guy started it."

"I don't care who started it, just pack up and go."

"Are you throwing him out, too?" I ask.

"I'll give you ten minutes and then I'll call the police."

We threw our stuff together as quickly as we could. Even though we were busy, Sam started squawking at me.

"For Chrissakes, was that necessary?"

"Yes, very."

"You know, if you're going to act this way, I don't even want to be around you."

Rather than continue the argument, I gave her the silent treatment. On the way out of the campground, my final statement was to rev my bike in front of the chubby hubby's metal palace. We were escorted to the gate by Ranger Rick.

When we started up the road toward town, to add to our misery, the skies opened up. We got back on Route 1 heading North. It was now about midnight and both of our asses were dragging. I could tell by the way that Sam was driving that she wanted to strangle me. I chose the path of least resistance and pulled into a low-level motel, finally putting an end to our lousy night.

The next day wasn't much better. The rain never let up. We saw a window of opportunity around noontime but three hours later, we hadn't covered much ground. Even though we were well into July, the rain brought a cold chill that rolled right through us as we were riding. We had to do another night in a low budget hotel before we reached Eastport.

The rain relented the next morning and we were on our way. We stayed in Eastport for two days. It was similar to Bar Harbor without the attitude. The weather was good enough so we were camping again. We decided it was time to move inland before we hit the Canadian border. We mapped out a route to the Rangely Lake area. I was familiar with Rangely from ski trips when I was a kid. It is also home to the Snowdeo, which is like Bike Week for snowmobilers. Stuck in the western mountains of Maine, Rangely is best known for its great fishing, moose, and Doc Grants, a notorious north country saloon.

It took us three days to get to Rangley. We stopped at the general store and inquired about places to stay. The man behind the register was a fountain of knowledge. When we told him we were looking for a campground, he steered us in a different direction.

He said, "I know this fella who owns a cabin right on the lake. It's nothing fancy but you can rent it almost as cheap as a campsite. It's even got outdoor plumbing."

"How do I get in touch with this fella?" I inquired.

"You're looking at him."

He gave us the key and directions and told us to go check the place out. The cabin was right on Moosalooktuck Lake. It was just one big room with a fireplace. There was a little camp stove in the corner and a big old feather bed. There was also a small table with two collapsible beach chairs. It had electricity but there were only two stand up lamps with no shades. These were on either end of a robin's egg blue naugahyde sofa. Although it was sparse, it seemed like a perfect place for our base camp. We headed back to the general store and closed the deal. That's when our landlord turned into a real Mainer and started tacking on all of the extras we would need for the week. The question and answer session got repititious real fast.

"Are you planning on doing any fishing?" he asked.

"Yeah, I'd love to but we don't have any gear."

"That's no problem, there's some down at the cabin. The

rent's two dollars a day. Do you have a fishing license?"

"No, I didn't even have a rod until a minute ago."

"Well, I just happen to have some here. Fifteen dollars for you and the missus. Are you planning on going out on the canoe?"

"Probably."

"That's five dollars a day. Would you like some supplies brought up there for you?"

"Yeah, let me guess, five bucks."

I now know how our new landlord makes all his cash. He hooks up some poor bastard with his cheap cabin and then slowly bleeds the prick with little add-ons.

For the first part of the week, Sam and I became comfortable in our surroundings, not leaving camp much. All we'd do was fish, swim, canoe, and screw. In the heat of the day we could lay out on a rock, perched right next to the lake. It was like a granite chaise lounge. And with no neighbors, there were no clothes.

By day four, we were becoming housebound and decided to scrap our nightly cookout. We went to Doc Grants for mooseburgers and beers. Docs claim to fame is being located exactly halfway between the equator and the North Pole. This happens to be bullshit but it's a great tagline. On one side there's a row of tables and on the other there's a long bar the length of the building. Every conceivable antler hangs from the walls and there's a row of pool tables separating the bar customers from the diners. The clientele is made up of loggers, fishermen, hunters, and locals looking for a good time. You can get just about anything you want including a wide, warm local prostitute if you feel the urge. Sam and I felt more at home among the working class. Bar Harbor seemed far away already.

We spent the rest of the week at the cabin. There was

really no reason to go anywhere else. Although my relationship with Sam seemed to be growing closer, my summer was growing shorter.

Our last day at the cabin I went down and picked up some bacon and eggs for breakfast. It was the first time I had touched any of that crap since I left the Honey Bee. Out of all the thousands of breakfasts I cooked, this is the first one I would eat myself.

While Sam was being treated to a full-scale breakfast, I browsed the local paper. A story about canoeing the Allagash caught my eye. I showed it to Sam and our next location was determined.

We left Rangely feeling nothing but great and took a day trip to Greenville, Maine. Greenville is located at the base of Moosehead Lake. Northern Outfitters is the company that specializes in wilderness trips through Moosehead Lake all the way to the Allagash River. As the crow flies, the trip can be as long as 100 miles.

After an overnight in Greenville, we got to the Northwoods first thing in the morning. Sam and I decided on a seven-day package so we could take in all of Moosehead and most of the Allagash wilderness waterway. They let us put our bikes in a barn and they set us up with all of the equipment we would need for our journey. We reviewed the map of their campsites that were located at 10-mile intervals throughout the lake and river system. Sam and I hit the lake early with every intention of plowing through as many miles as we could that first day. We quickly realized that our canoeing skills were less than perfect. We got to the first camp and our arms were about to fall off. We enjoyed a charming dinner that evening of pepperoni crackers and gingersnaps. That first night we began to realize how alone we were. The only noise we could hear was the slap of the water against the shore. The night sky was endlessly deep. The only reminder of civilization was an occasional lonely plane in the sky.

We broke camp the next morning with the intention of taking on most of Moosehead that day. After two hours, we reluctantly accepted that that was impossible and set our sights a little lower. We focused on a campsite on one of the many islands on the lake. Our arms were slowly getting stronger and we reached the island earlier than expected. Sam set up camp and I thought I'd make an attempt at catching us dinner. I had no such luck. The delicious meal of trout was instead beef jerky, granola bars, and filtered water.

The next day was hard paddling but we finished up Moosehead. We landed in North East Carry at the north end of the lake around noon. We grabbed dinner and headed to Seboomook for the night. We set up a makeshift rotisserie and grilled two small chickens. While they were roasting away, we enjoyed some Canadian Whiskey and smokes that we had picked up in North East Carry. We weren't sure if the chickens were actually cooked, but the smell was so intoxicating we inhaled the two birds.

We were now comfortably fat and stupid. I mentioned to Sam how strange it was that we had chosen this route, rather than concentrating on easier locales with amenities. We kept getting deeper into the forest the further we went on our trip.

"I can feel everything about myself starting to change. The guy who was wired to his business and pressure was left behind about Rangely. The person who could barely camp for the night is feeling a lot more at home in the wild. When I left this time, I dreamed that I could take on the road one more time. I'm now just about convinced of it."

"Won't you miss having a home," Sam asked.

"No, I've had that before, a couple of times. I always felt like an alien in that world. I don't know why I worked so hard to attain it. I feel like I was meant to be nomadic. I know that at some point being a wanderer would take me out. I wonder how long it would take before the bike or roaming around would do me in."

"That doesn't sound like much of a life."

"It does to me. I never wanted to end up in a nursing home drooling on myself, anyway. I don't look at death as a curse, just a final agonizing statement."

Sam didn't have much to say but I got the feeling she was thinking more and more about home. I think Sam believed that she had one more shot at a home, apple pie, and a hubby. I no longer had any such delusions. I could also feel my physical nature changing. I had dropped a few pounds and drinking was now an occasion instead of a lifestyle. Internally, I felt like I was detoxifying. The stress and agitation inside me was now replaced by day-to-day survival. I had given up my role as aggressor and am now content with being an observer.

As Sam and I headed up the Allagash for the second half of the trip, I felt I was well on my way to my rebirth. We landed at Clayton Lake on the seventh day to catch a shuttle back to Greenville. The ride took a long four hours, some of the roads were old logging trails. I could count the number of cars we saw on two hands. Pulling into Greenville, it felt like we were entering a metropolis.

We got a motel room in Greenville for the night. It felt good to wash a week's camping out of us. That night we mapped out the next leg of our trip. The direction brought us toward New Hampshire. We both knew the ultimate destination was Rutland but neither of us said a word about it.

Leaving Greenville, we rode south. Each little town was

marked by a convenience store, gas pump, and post office. The roads were tight and ragged from frost heaves and logging trucks. We could barely top forty mph, which turned out to be lucky for Sam. Just as we were leaving the small town of Harmony, after gassing up, the thing that you never think will happen, did. There was a small intersection at the bottom of a hill. Sam and I had the right of way. I was in front and Sam was about thirty feet behind me. Out of the corner of my eye, I saw a car approaching the intersection to my left. He had a stop sign so I didn't think anything of it. I just assumed he'd stop.

Then there came that noise, there was no screeching of brakes, only a crunching sound, then a grinding that only metal can make when being dragged along pavement. I knew immediately what had happened. For a split second I didn't want to turn around, fearing the worst. I hit my brakes and slid to a stop. I turned back and saw Sam lying on her side, squirming in pain. It seemed to take too long to get back to her even though it was only a few seconds. Her motorcycle was lying in the middle of the road about fifteen feet from her. It looked like the whole back end had been taken off. I just hoped she looked better than her bike.

I finally reached Sam and the first thing I noticed was that her leg was twisted and bleeding. She was conscious but quiet. I pulled her visor up from her helmet. Before I could utter a word, she said, "it's my leg. It just fucking hurts."

Right at that second, I could hear the unmistakable sound of a logging truck off in the distance. The old fool that hit Sam was still sitting in his car just shaking his head. I felt obligated to go over and scream at him but it was more important to take care of Sam first.

"Do you have a phone?" I yelled at the man.

He shook his head and said, "Let me go get help."

"Hurry," I screamed back.

Just as he was getting ready to take off, the logging truck came down upon us. The driver jumped out of his cab and asked if he could help. Luckily, he had a phone and he called 911. They assured him that an ambulance would be on the way. There was one in Athens and it would get there in about ten minutes.

I quickly turned my attention back to Sam. She seemed to be shivering so I grabbed my sleeping bag off my bike and covered her up. As I was putting it on her she turned to lay flat and I could see a bone protruding from the top of her left leg. It seemed to be gushing a little more blood so I took my belt and slipped it around the top of her leg creating a makeshift tourniquet. Sam responded to my attempt at playing doctor with a long, painful moan.

I apologized and she said, "Take my helmet off." I started to undo the strap to her helmet when the old fool who hit her advised me that I shouldn't move her until the ambulance got there. Before I had a chance to answer him, I could hear the distant wail of sirens. It seemed to take forever but they finally got there and the police were right behind them. They quickly got Sam secured on a backboard to protect her neck and then slid her on a stretcher. Once they started to take her over to the ambulance, the deputy came over and told me that I needed to give a statement. I told him that I was going to the hospital but he assured me that Sam's injuries were not life threatening and he'd make sure I made it to the hospital shortly.

Before they put Sam in the ambulance, he let me go over and talk with her quickly. I told her she'd be all right and I'd be with her at the hospital as soon as I could.

I gave my statement and a tow truck came and picked up Sam's bike. The sheriff was finally done with us and he gave me directions to the Redington Fairview Hospital in Skowhegan.

Racing to the hospital, all I could think about was the sound of the collision. Sam had had her helmet on but what if it had been me? Could I reach an early demise that quickly? I wonder how it would have felt if that old bastard had been two seconds earlier. Would there be a white light, a warm glow, or just a deep dark pit? There's one thing I did know, I'm glad it was her and not me.

When I got to the hospital, Sam was in surgery. The nurse told me that the leg was in pretty rough shape but with surgery and therapy she'd be able to walk just fine. She didn't seem to have any other serious injuries expect for scrapes and cuts.

THE NEXT week was hell, but I owed it to Sam to make sure she got home and was feeling okay. I stayed at a motel in Skowhegan and visited her each day. It took a couple of days until she was up on crutches. Then they started her physical therapy. By the end of the week, she was ready to be released.

I rented a small Ryder box van and put my bike and what was left of Sam's inside. Before I went to pick up Sam at the hospital, I decided to call Emily from my motel room. The summer was rapidly spinning to a conclusion and I had promised her a call. I caught her before she left for work. She seemed surprised to hear from me. I asked her how everything was going and she gave me a little laundry list like she was an anchor on the six o'clock news. Everything seemed okay, the Honey Bee was holding up, the kids were good. The real question was, how was Emily? Was she in the throes of love? Was the Professor sitting over in my chair petting Caesar or did the fucking egghead run out of Viagra? I didn't ask and the conversation ended when I told her I'd see her around Labor Day.

I left for the hospital to pick up Sam and we began our eight-hour trip to Rutland. It was a long quiet ride there. I could see Sam thinking about how to cut the strings. Except for a stop to gas up and get a little food, we just kept moving toward Rutland. Sam's mother had a small cape on the outskirt of town and she was pretty friendly to me considering all that had happened. Sam's Mom insisted that I stay there for the night. I accepted because I still had to get Sam's motorcycle stored and drop off the rental truck. By the time I completed those missions, I went right to sleep, thinking about my escape the next morning.

Sam's mother went to work early and Sam made coffee before I left.

"Thanks for taking care of me after the accident. You made things a lot easier. I really enjoyed our trip. I'm going to miss you."

"It's been great but it's time for you to go chase those dreams."

We gave each other a kiss goodbye and I headed out to my motorcycle. As I drove off in no particular direction, I did know one thing; six weeks might be my limit with women before my nature of being disinterested takes over.

I LEFT RUTLAND with Montreal in mind so I headed north up Route 7. After about an hour, I stopped in Brandon where my other sister Carol had lived. I stopped at the lake where I had visited her about twenty years earlier. I was up there with my first wife and my kids. My sister had seemed to be enjoying life in rural Vermont with her family intact and the future ahead of her. We spent the day at a public beach in the middle of the Green Mountains. I stood there thinking about how happy she was that day. I needed to remember her like that instead of in the pain of depression that finally did her in.

I continued on Route 7 north up until Charlotte where I

decided to take a ferry across Lake Champlain into the Adirondacks. I ended up sleeping by the side of the road outside Plattsburg, New York. In one day I had left Sam, saw where my sister had her best times, and then saw where Sam had her worst.

By noon the next day I was back in Montreal. I picked a dumpy little motel outside of St. Catherine's Street to plot my return home. Before I got down to some heavy thinking, I thought it was time to do some heavy drinking. The exchange rate was so good I could have stayed there for a month but they'd have to take me out in a body bag.

The next couple days were a little blurry. I kept to myself during the day but in the evening I would go down to St. Catherine's Street and just be fully entertained. The strippers were still there but regrettably they looked like their American counterparts, all juiced up with silicone and shaved like Vin Diesel. The lax drug laws of Canada also offered ample opportunity to sample some good hashish. This added to the glow of the city of festivals.

I could tell I was getting older because after a couple days St. Catherine's Street bored me. I decided to take a ride along the St. Lawrence River. After a couple of hours, I landed in Trois Rivieres. There was a little watering hole there overlooking the river. There were some motorcycles in the parking lot so I figured it would be a good stop. Their license plates were from British Colombia. I was just in the infancy of my trip, these guys were 2,500 miles from home.

It only took us a couple of minutes to get acquainted. These four guys were from Vancouver. They had been friends since they were kids. This was their dream trip; they had taken six weeks off to do all of Canada. Their plan was to hit the Atlantic in one more day, then turn around and head back. They would then conduct the rest of their lives in some sort of normal fashion. They asked me who I was and what I was doing up in Canada. It was more important for me to tell them where I was going. I said that I was officially a drop out. I was going to continue my journey forever or until I got scraped off the road. I would go from place to place at my whim, work enough to get by, get close to being comfortable, then pack up and leave. I was really going everywhere, there was no place I couldn't go. I would never fall in love again, there would only be short intervals of companionship.

As I was telling these total strangers what my plans were, I realized that they actually excited me. I knew though that in a week or so I'd have to return home and make the final cut.

I LEFT MONTREAL with a plan and slowly worked my way back home. I was now camping out every night and as each day went on, my plan and my rules became clearer. The territory became more familiar as I got nearer to the seacoast and I could feel the tension building for my visit back to the world that used to own me.

I pulled into Portsmouth and went over to see Jason to continue the visual story that was growing on my chest. Jason kept my books of hieroglyphics up on his shelf. I brought him up to date on how my life was turning. In three hours, the second row was done and I was ready to go out and discover the third.

THE NEW TATTOOS were still stinging and I had to give Emily a call. I stopped into the Muddy River for some bottled bravery and used their payphone. It was hard to dial the numbers. I wasn't sure what I would find. Was the Professor all moved in and comfy? Would she be shocked that I was going to leave again? Emily is the last woman I will ever love. She deserves better than me.

After three feeble attempts, I finally found some magical way to dial the numbers. I got the answering machine and half-way through my fumbling, foolish message, she picked up the phone. I told her I was in the area and I needed to see her when-ever she could squeeze me in. She asked if I had anywhere to stay. I told her not yet. She told me to come over to the house and have some supper. To my surprise, she also said I could stay at the house.

When I pulled in the driveway, the house looked exactly the same as when I left. Emily did have a nice new kayak on top of her Volvo. I could see the neighbors peering out the window thinking, "Oh shit, he's back."

Emily had heard the motorcycle and met me at the door. "My God, you look different."

She was right, I did. The only problem was, in my mirror, I had only gotten better.

"What's the matter, you didn't take a razor with you?"

I hadn't shaved since Montreal so a short beard was added to my long goatee. I was looking pretty scruffy.

"Do you mind if I clean up before dinner?" I asked.

"Course not, the house is still half yours," she said. I won-dered for how long. Emily said she'd be cooking some chicken on the grill and to take my time.

Half an hour later, we were sitting outside at the picnic table, devouring dinner. It was almost hard to start the conver-sation, so I began with a question that I never asked often enough.

"Emily, how have you been doing? Is everything okay?"

"Everything's good. I've been wrapped up at work. I went to the Cape with my mother and sister a few weeks ago."

"How was your trip to Nova Scotia?"

"It was okay. The scenery was beautiful. I met a lot of interesting people in my field. In fact, there's another seminar in Washington put on by the Smithsonian coming up in November."

"Sounds like things are going in the right direction for you. Have you heard anything from Guy?"

"No, but I've been cashing the checks. So tell me about your summer."

"Bike Week was great, but looking back, I think the rest of the summer was better. I did a lot of camping, a little fishing, not too much drinking. I now know every stop in Maine from the Allagash to Eastport. I saw the Green Mountains, the White Mountains, the Adirondacks. I visited Sweden, Naples, Athens, and Poland and the only thing I found out was that there's a lot more to see."

She gave me that Emily look where she kind of squints and the corner of her mouth drops a bit. This is usually an indication that she's not happy with something I've said. "So I take it your not going to stick around."

Normally I would give her the answer that I thought she wanted to hear, but after all my years of lying, why bother? "No, that's what I came here to talk about."

"Well, what are you going to do?"

"I don't really know but for a while I'll probably travel south. I don't think I'll be settling in any place in particular. What does your future look like?"

"With the job, I'll probably stay right here. This is home for me and I'd like to keep it that way."

"I'd like you to stay here, too."

Surprisingly, the negotiations were going well. Emily looked good and her new life seemed to suit her. She wondered aloud how long I would be able to keep up the lifestyle of roaming around. I told her it wasn't the length of time that mattered but the quality. I also told her to go with life as she chose, I would not interrupt. I owed her that.

Everything was going well but we kept avoiding the "d" word. It was finally brought up at the end of our dinner.

"Emily, I hate to ask this question, but would you want a divorce?"

"Does it matter?"

"No. You're the last wife I'll ever have. You've given me so much. No man could ask for more. I will still love you forever. My soul will always be yours, even if my spirit is on the road."

We kissed and just smiled at one another till the sun started its descent. Emily told me that I was still her guy and divorce was not in the picture. I was dying to ask about the Professor, but at this point, I realized it was no longer my business. I did get the feeling that Emily was finding the contentment she'd always craved.

As AWKWARD as it was, we just left it at that. I told her that I'd be in touch periodically and that I'd stop back next summer to take care of any business.

Strangely enough, Emily and I had a great night. She even let me sleep in her bed. Our bodies were still the perfect match, even if our paths were headed in different directions. Emily was still the best lover I've ever had. Maybe we were both thinking, What the hell? This could be the last time.

The next morning was time to break camp. She had to go to work and I had to go visit another woman. Even though we were still in love, we left each other like we were old friends, just a quick kiss and a silent respect for our choices.

I felt pretty good about leaving. It was so different from

when I had left a few months ago for Laconia. Now, I'm look-ing forward. I still had two more stops before moving on: the Honey Bee and Joe's Playland.

The Honey Bee never changes. The parking lot was still loaded. I could smell bacon and eggs as I drove in the lot. All the customers were still in their assigned seats and Regina did a triple-take before she realized it was me. Guy just stood there in my spot. I think he was a little grayer than when I left. He seemed as miserable as I used to be.

"Guy man, how are you doing?"

"I'm good, business is good, but Jesus, you never told me you had to work this hard."

"Stop bitching, you look great. All the labor is paying off. I love the new goatee, it gives you a rougher edge."

Guy rolls his eyes and says, "You need that edge for this place."

"So, did I miss anything over the summer?"

"Yeah. Rotha's busband pulled a gun on Leon and Rotha when they were going at it in Leon's vani n the parking lot."

"I hope that dumb bastard shot them both."

"No, but he did end up shooting himself in the foot."

That's what I miss most about the Honey Bee: there is never a day that goes by that doesn't make you feel a little more normal than the rest of the world.

"A little birdy told me you were waking up at the crack of dawn. Is that Honey Bee fact or fiction?" I ask.

"Let's just say she's keeping an eye on me," Guy answers.

"The good one, I hope?" I never understood Guy's pro-clivity for women with a lazy eye but what the hell do I know? I once dated a woman because she could yodel.

I was really proud of Guy. I could tell he had grown into his new role even though the worry lines of being boss were now creasing his forehead. I told him not to worry, in another ten years he could get a motorcycle and live like a bum. I could tell he was doing well. I wished him the best and then got out of there before he could put an apron on me.

Then there was only one more stop to make. I figured I had to go back to Salisbury to check in with the Gypsy Woman. I wanted to let her know that I took her advice. I made the slow turn up the Salisbury strip, the only parking spot was in front of the Normandy due to the Labor Day crowds. I squeezed my bike in between three others that were clustered out front. I walked over to Joe's, expecting to have another question answered. I went to the spot where I'd stood many times before and was shocked at what I saw. The gypsy woman was gone. In her place was a Mortal Kombat video arcade game. The manager informed me he had sold the gypsy woman for $35,000. He said she had been a one-of-a-kind antique. She was worth every penny. I wonder if the new owner was letting her practice her trade or if she was bought by some collector who had her stuffed in a crate, waiting for a quick buck.

As shocked as I was, it was just another sign that the Sailsbury I loved was dying a slow, painful death. The bars I once frequented were being replaced by seaside condos, fit for some gold-chained guido. The Bowery was now Tens, the Kon-Tiki was boarded up, and The Frolics was demolished. The giant wooden rollercoaster that once towered over the beach was a vacant lot. My true beach home was now just a shell of its grand past. Where entire families once prowled the busy beach for a week at a time, there was now only a ghost town with trash serving as tumbleweed.

I left Joe's Playland for the last time, there were no more answers for me there. My disappointment brought me to the Normandy where I lamented the loss of my mentor as I also celebrated her years of good advice. Maybe the disappearance of the Gypsy Woman was her way of letting me go.

The tall necks gathered in front of me just like old times. I was daydreaming about where my next stop would be. I was awoken from my deep thought by a drunk who stumbled into my stool. My look said, screw you.

"What the fuck are you looking at, Motorcycle Man?" the drunk slurred. The old fool stumbled against the wall before he walked away to bother someone else. I looked around the Normandy and all I could see was a bunch of sad old men with sadder stories. I was sitting there with them but the difference was that the next day I'd be gone. Tomorrow might be better. They'll always be sitting on the same stool.

I got on my bike ready to leave the gypsy, Salisbury, and the Normandy for good. I wasn't really sure where I was going. But I was now looking forward rather than back. As I stopped at the light in Salisbury center, I noticed a car in front of me had Louisiana plates. Fate decided my destination. It's been nearly twenty years since I'd been to the Crescent City. New Orleans might be the best place to start my new life.

THE END

Next from Motorcycleman...

Voodoo Moon

Chapter One:
Lost and Found

My freedom is finally at hand as I begin the slow crawl south down US Route 1. All the history, stress, and lost dreams were all left at the last stop light. My big bear of a bike now feels weightless. The road is like black silk. The typical roar of the highway is replaced by the Zen-like hum of contentment. For me, this is a perfect moment. No doubts linger about my choices. The blind optimism of youth that I experienced on my first cross-country trip is creeping back into my middle-aged mind.

This dream state has quickly delivered me to the Newburyport Bridge and my final exit from Salisbury. The slow rise to the crest of the bridge unveils the old haunts of a life that seems far away. The Black Cow's deck is full of couples toasting a warm September afternoon. I wonder if they are as happy as Emily and I were. I bear down on my throttle for a little extra help to leave these thoughts behind.

By the time I clear the bridge and hit the underpass, I am officially at Mach One. As I approach the stop light ahead, I can tell by the opposing traffic that the light is about to change. It is an easy choice. Ripping through the yellow light, I notice the unmarked cruiser to my left. It is too late to even give a token effort to slow down. Without turning my head, I give a quick look in my back mirror and see him turn in my direction.

He has given me a quarter of a mile and he disappears behind a small hill before turning on his lights. My decision is quick, before he can catch another glimpse of me, I slide into the back of a convenience store. Barely coming to a stop, I peek out to the road and see Robocop go screaming by lit up like a trailer park on Christmas Eve. I give him a quick tip of my helmet as the siren starts to fade into misdirection. I can only wonder what disaster he was rushing to?

This is a good chance to change my route. I backtrack and start to head out of Newburyport feeling that victory is mine. The rush of winning is short-lived as a patrol car passes in the opposite direction and pulls a quick u-turn. This time there is no escape. I pull over and sneak a tic-tac mouthwash out of my pocket to combat any smell the Normandy might have left. I start to prepare the necessary paper-work as another cruiser pulls in front of me. I hear a familiar siren and now my friend the secret agent is blocking my bike.

Each one of the blue knights has a twinkle in his eye. The detective that I eluded is the first to approach. He isn't real tall and he has a soft gut that hangs over the only stiff thing about him, a glock which he begins to stroke like a thirteen year old. The other uniforms circle around at a safe distance. As if I didn't know I was officially screwed, the detective is the legendary Dave Farley who never met a motorcy-clist he didn't hate, ticket, and harass.

His first words confirm the depth of my dilemma. "Have you had anything to drink today?"

Rather than shut my mouth, this dick deserves an answer. "Defi-nitely not enough," I say.

He is not amused. "Go over to the car and put your hands on the hood."

The other cops watch in joy as Farley gives me a pat down, takes the registration out of my hand, and cuffs me. "Do you have a li-cense?"

"It's in my wallet." He pulls the wallet out of my back pocket and has a bitch of a time unclipping it off of the chain. His effort is rewarded when he opens it up observing a fresh bunch of Benjamins, my license, and a pack of easy widers. One of the uniforms comes over and puts me in the back of detective shithead's car then goes back and joins the conference around my bike. After a quick call to head-quarters, they begin to toss through my bike and I have to recall all the goodies they might find. The knife is barely legal. The Marijuana isn't. The derringer is okay in New Hampshire, but not in the land of the Kennedy's. Luckily I hid that under my seat in a chrome box that looks more like equipment than a holster.

Their concentration is on my saddlebags and I can feel the high fives as they find a couple of joints I had rolled for emergencies. They are also intrigued by the amount of traveler's checks along with the cash they found.

Detective Farley walks back over to the cruiser and reads me my rights. I can only think how quickly things have changed. The taste of freedom and the beginning of my new destiny was short lived. But I would do anything to get it back.

Visit the world of Motorcycleman at www.motocycle-man.com, for products, calendar, characters, and a peak into the future.

Phil Englehart, creator of the *Motorcycleman* series, is a throwback to the era of street-smart writers. Just as Kerouac and Bukowsky understood the dissatisfaction of the "Beat generation," Mr. Englehart crawls into the psyche of the boomers mid-life torments.

His work history has been Zelig-like, including fisherman, carnival hawker, columnist, restaurant owner, construction foreman, and fortune teller. In between occupations he has crossed the country twice on his motorcycle. *Motorcycleman: Restless* was written entirely on butcher paper in the back of his donut shop. Mr. Englehart is still slinging hash in southern New Hampshire where he currently lives with his beautiful wife, Kate, and his dog, Caesar.